Henry's Version

ALSO BY BRETT SHAPIRO

Late in the Day

Those around Him

l'Intruso
(in Italian only)

Bailey Strikes It Rich
(in French, German and Korean only)

The Adventures of Bailey the Bag Dog
(in French and German only)

Nourishing the Land, Nourishing the People
(also in French)

Regenerating Forests and Livelihoods

Henry's Version

a novel

Brett Shapiro

atmosphere press

Grateful acknowledgment is made to Farrar, Strauss and Giroux for permission to reprint an excerpt of the poem "Aubade" by Philip Larkin, from *The Complete Poems of Philip Larkin*, edited by Archie Burnett.

...The mind blanks at the glare. Not in remorse
—The good not done, the love not given, time
Torn off unused—nor wretchedly because
An only life can take so long to climb
Clear of its wrong beginning, and may never;
But at the total emptiness for ever,
The sure extinction that we travel to
And shall be lost in always. Not to be here,
Not to be anywhere,
And soon; nothing more terrible, nothing more true...

From "Aubade" – Philip Larkin, 1977

BOOK ONE

One

Am I?" I asked my mother when I was twelve. Or thirteen. I don't remember. I'm not even sure that I actually asked her. I do remember her eyes, though. They didn't shy away from looking directly into mine whenever I talked to her about things I thought might make her angry. I liked to look at them back. But not this time.

My best friend Donny told me he'd asked his mom the same question. "You know what she had to say?" he said. "She said, 'No.' That's it. Like I was asking her something that she always said no to. Like, 'Can I drive the car up and down the driveway to practice?' But then she squeezed me so hard I forgot it was supposed to be a hug. Cripes."

Donny looked like his mom—red hair, pale skin, face flecked with freckles, straight eyebrows that barely had a space between them. That he would ask her such a question seemed stupid to me. So stupid that he didn't really ask her at all, that he was just trying to "relate" when I told him I wondered whether I was adopted.

We continued playing tetherball in his large back yard. As hard as I smacked the ball with my open fist to make it coil tightly around the pole, the question stuck to me like the sticky strips that the adults in the neighborhood hung on their front porches in summer to catch flying insects with. We kids gathered around the strips to watch a variety of bugs as they ripped their legs off trying to free themselves from the amber-colored glue.

"Look at those fly strips," my mother would say. "Like Shirley Temple curls, except they kill."

My mother, Edith, spent hours tending to her thick waves of jet-black hair. She talked a lot about her hair too, and used the word "unruly" so much that I assumed it was a normal everyday word. She had a fixed appointment every two weeks at the beauty parlor with Delores, the owner.

"I love the way she gets rid of the dead ends," she said to me if she happened to be coming through the back door after her appointment while I was in the kitchen rummaging for a snack, preferably a bag of beer pretzels or cheese curls. "She takes small sections of hair and twists them between her fingers until they're tight like a twig, and then she passes her Bic lighter up and down the twig to burn off the hair ends that stick out. The ones that are split in two. The dead ends. All that death on my head. What a stink." She'd go about her usual business, fluffing her hair up with her hands to make Delores's creation last longer.

I didn't notice any difference. To me she looked the same, and I wondered why she made these biweekly appointments with Delores. The other mothers in the neighborhood didn't look that much different when they came back from the beauty parlor either. Most of them went to Delores, too. I didn't get all the fuss and didn't care. Every time my mother returned, she was perky and carefree. I could count on it. It was comforting to be able to count on certain things happening, especially when they had to do with happiness.

My father, Marvin, had thin, dirty blond hair, which he rushed his comb through each morning without looking in the mirror. He didn't go to a barber shop. My mother cut his hair. "I can take care of it at home," she announced at the dinner table as she showed us a hair-styling kit she'd seen advertised on television for a one-time-only discount rate and set it beside the fruit salad that she'd made for dessert. "He has simple hair."

My father looked at her with a blank expression. "Is that fresh pineapple in there?" he asked her. "The chunks are irregular."

"Let's give you a haircut tonight," she'd say to him every month or so, as she was clearing the dessert plates. "Your neck is like a gorilla's."

"I'm all yours." My father would retreat to his recliner and sit back in the fully horizontal position with the headrest down while she landscaped his head, experimenting with each of the five plastic attachments encased in the Styrofoam packaging. She'd gotten her money's worth. He was silent throughout the enterprise—except that first time when she got so carried away he ended up with a buzz cut. "Sweetheart," he said when she gave him the hand-mirror to inspect, "my Army days are over. You've butchered me. What the hell!" He got up from his chair and stormed out of the room. I'd never seen the shape of his head without hair, which resembled a lemon, never heard him curse before, and never thought him capable of such a display of vanity as he skulked down the hallway, raking his fingers through his bristly head with the horror and fury of someone who'd been exposed in a private place. Who was this man?

"Dad?" I called out. He didn't respond. When I heard him slam the door to the bathroom, I wondered whether he'd still be the same man I counted on him being when he returned to the family room. Donny made me wonder things like that too, stuff about whether love could be relied on or whether it was a temporary boost, like the way my mother poured it on after she went to Delores.

My older sister, Adrienne, had hair that was thick like our mother's, straight like our father's, and a color that was the perfect blend of Mom and Dad's. Leave it to her to play both sides.

"Mousy brown," I told her one night in the bathroom as I waited for her to finish combing her hair so she'd leave and I could take a pee. The second bathroom was downstairs and I was too lazy to make the trip. The third bathroom was the exclusive domain of my parents. No children allowed.

"Creep. What do you know?"

"How about dark dirty-blonde?"

"Gross."

"I give up. What color is your hair?"

"Chestnut."

"Chestnut? Like the hutch in the dining room? You're already built like furniture, sis."

She grabbed my hand, led me to her bedroom, and pointed to the *Seventeen* magazine on her bed. "Look," she said.

I picked up the magazine. The cover photo was of a woman lying on the beach, her privates covered by seaweed and her long hair working its way through the sand like scavenging tentacles. The other parts of her body were fleshy, curvy and sinewy.

"Like hers," she said. "Sexy."

"Like her what? She's sexy everywhere."

"What do you know about sexy?"

I tried to feel what I'd just said course through my smooth and hairless sapling of a body. It didn't work, except when my thoughts shifted to the Sears catalog and its images of men clad in all-cotton briefs. "Sexy" worked there. There I felt heat.

The model did have the same color hair as Adrienne, which was the same color as the hutch in the dining room that was my grandmother's. Adrienne moved her left index finger along the caption under the photo. "See?" she said. "Chestnut. It says it right there." She lifted her hand from the page to caress the long straight locks on the left side of her head.

I dropped the magazine and headed out of her room. "Gotta pee."

Adrienne's eyes were a blend of my parents' too—the

dark brown of our mother's folded into the blue-gray of our father's. When Adrienne tried on the navy green sweater our mother knitted for her, Mom said, "It goes with your lovely hazel eyes." Hazel? Such a strange word for a color. My mother gently passed her hand down the contours of Adrienne's freckled cheek and continued down to the left sleeve of the sweater, smoothing the mohair along the way. I observed the gesture, took note of the word she was using in a new and undecipherable way, and felt estranged from the codes and strokings of family. I had to have been adopted. The fact that my hair was red didn't help. It wasn't as fiery red as Donny's. Still, I was the one everyone in school called "Reds." How he managed to avoid being the one called Reds was beyond me. It probably had to do with him being cool and sure of himself despite his hair. Someone not to mess with. Someone to easily fall in love with. He was my best friend. I didn't see him all that much, but he was on my mind all the time. I hoped I was on his too.

"THE COUNTER MAN at the delicatessen—Indian, but he's nice."

"The colored guy down the street bought a Cutlass Supreme. How'd he manage that?"

"Phyllis was sitting on the patio last night for three hours. I could hear the ice in her whiskey glass clinking the whole time. Not married, poor thing. And such a lush."

My mother prided herself on her observations of the locals. I soaked in what she had to say in the way a dry sponge absorbs any water that lands on it. When I was twelvish, her observations weren't so permeable anymore. I questioned them. "What do you mean, Mom?"

And when I asked her what she meant, her face screwed up and she got all surly and dismissive. "What do you want from me, for Chrissake? I'm just a Philly girl."

She was born and raised in a Jewish ghetto in north Philly.

The main artery—Marshall Street—was an eruption of store-fronts, pushcarts and languages. Pike, apples, ice, awls, schmat-tas. Everyone had something to sell; everyone needed some-thing to buy. Clutter and chaos. Life. In the back room of each store was a steep, dimly lit stairway leading up to the sec-ond floor, where the store owner and assorted family mem-bers lived. The side streets were considered the suburbs, since the rows of two-story units had no storefront on the ground floor. "The awnings above the jalousie windows were kept clean, and some houses had pots of geraniums by the front door," she told me. "The flowers didn't last long. It was a great idea. But people were too busy making a living to think about watering a pot of flowers." She didn't miss a chance to tell me how, after school and long into the night, she stayed in my grandfather's produce shop to help him before going upstairs to do her homework. "I liked to polish and stack the fruit in the display window into pyramids. I wanted to make it per-fect, a work of art. So untouchable that customers would want to come in to touch it. To help sales, you know. Such hard times they were." A flicker of the American dream could be felt along those streets and in that shop, at least the way she told it, especially when she went on and on about the harsh conditions and persistent hope and ended by fanning her arms, like a male peacock does with its feathers, to indicate the spacious living room of our house. "And now look. Look what we have here. Who could've thought?" I didn't under-stand what the big deal was. The living room looked more or less like the ones everyone else in the neighborhood had. What was the big deal? Donny's was much bigger. His parents entertained.

Our living room sofa was L-shaped and glazed with thick plastic slipcovers. There was little that the sofa needed to be protected from, since our living room was a dead zone, reserved for the company that didn't happen in our house except when Aunt Leah, Uncle Morris and my three first cousins came for Thanksgiving dinner. Even then, we kids spent most of our daylight hours in the rec room or roaming the neighborhood, the women in the kitchen preparing dinner, and the men in the yard doing whatever it was that men did in yards. Only after we finished our dinner in the dining room, the second-most unused room in the house, and brought our plates to the kitchen sink were all of us instructed by the women to go to the living room, where dessert would be served. My cousins and I sat cross-legged around the low round coffee table positioned in front of the inside angle where the two sides of the L met. The sofa itself was reserved for the adults. "Careful you don't make a mess," my mother warned my cousins and me as she handed us the can of Reddi-wip to decorate the top of our slices of pie. "And don't overdo it with the whipped cream."

My father and Uncle Morris sat on the short side of the sofa, which jutted into the living room itself. "Don't want your greasy heads leaving marks on the wall," my mother fussed. Uncle Morris was bald and sweated a lot. My father applied Brylcreem to his hair each morning before he hurried his brush through it.

My mother and Aunt Leah sat on the long side of the sofa. The sofa back had a slight incline, and the long side brushed against the wall, where it would be natural for a head to rest. My mother and her sister weren't the type to lean back and relax. They had to keep an eye on all that was happening around them to make sure that everything was just right. Even though the long side gave them plenty of room to spread out, they sat close, speaking to each other continually and in hushed tones. I couldn't make out a word they were saying. I guess that was the point.

When dessert was finished, everyone rose to carry their plates to the kitchen sink and then dispersed. No one returned to the living room, except when the relatives left and my mother went back to tidy up and restore it to being the most beautiful and unlived-in room in the house. Until the following Thanksgiving, it served no purpose other than as a thruway from the kitchen to the four stairs finishing at the bedroom hallway. You could see the well-worn route etched in the wall-to-wall carpeting.

The narrow triangle of tunnel created behind the sloped back of the sofa and the vertical wall was snug but filled with light coming from the picture window. The carpeting there was still plush. It was the ideal place to disappear to if ever I found the need for my parents to suffer deeply because of a gross injustice they'd subjected me to. They would never think to look for me there. I could slink into that embrasure like a dying animal and hide until I decided the time was right for me to crawl out and put an end to the despair my disappearance would have caused them. It might last forever, which might serve them right.

I'd emerge eventually.

"Thank God you're here!"

"We were so worried. We almost called the police!"

The tunnel was a place that could be used only once. I refused to be a boy who cried wolf. I had to choose carefully.

AT SCHOOL, NONE of the other students made fun of me. None of them gravitated toward me either. I kept my excellent grades a secret and made sure to wear penny loafers, although they weren't Weejuns and they cramped my toes. I had a modest selection of crew- and V-neck sweaters that matched my socks. Matching colors was the important factor, thank goodness, since my sweaters were bought in outlets, where their labels had been snipped off before they were dumped into the bargain bins that my mother forced me to burrow through with her. I also had a gold initial ring, which I insisted on for my bar mitzvah birthday. "Just this one tiny present. Please," I begged my parents. "No clothes. No games.

Nothing else." When my mother handed me the tiny single gift-wrapped box, I tore open the wrapping paper and opened the lid of the box. There it was, minus my middle initial.

"Where's the 'E'?" I asked. My middle name was Eli. I hated it.

"Be grateful we paid for two letters, Henry," my mother said. "Highway robbery. Fourteen karat gold, no less."

I turned the ring between my thumb and index finger. The "H" and the "R" created sufficient width without the "E," which would have made the ring spell "HER." No. Not so great after all.

"Thanks Mom. Thanks Dad." Maybe the missing "E" would go unnoticed at school and I could ease my way into the "in" crowd.

My clothes were unremarkable, but my grades were top-notch—straight As on my report cards, year after year. They came easy for me, but I couldn't let on to anyone at school. Having grades that were too good barred entrance to the in crowd. The popular kids didn't ask about grades. They wouldn't have much to brag about when it came to academic achievement, so they came to an agreement that grades had to be for losers. When the report cards were placed on our desks at the end of the day, I sweated to make my face expressionless as my eyes traveled down the predictable column of perfection. I kept my face down until the bell rang, waiting for the noise of the students shuffling out of the room to be thinned to a sporadic footstep or two before I made my exit. Only once was I stopped in the hallway and interrogated. By Donny. Mr. Popularity. Mr. Unattainable.

"How'd you do?" he asked.

I had no idea why he stopped to ask me. Why would he care about me and my grades?

"Pretty good," I said. "How about you?" His socks were the same color as the ones I'd worn the day before.

"The usual. Great sweater, by the way." He raised his left

arm and moved it until his hand rested gently on my shoulder. I tried to feel it through my sweater but couldn't. "Maybe come by after school sometime. You're down the street from me, right? We can hang out."

I was about to say, "How about after school today?" but as he withdrew his hand I went cold. I also realized that I would never be able to show up at his door unannounced, say "Hey" when he opened it, and embark on the life I was meant to live, coupled with the most coveted boy in the school.

"Sure." I didn't take up his offer. I never would. It wasn't in me.

AFTER A COUPLE of years of wearing clothes that barely crossed over into acceptance and keeping my brainiac grades a secret, I was confident that I was inconspicuous and that no one would bug me while I struggled to figure out where and how I fit in. In the meantime, I was half in and half out, which was exactly where I wanted to be, since I still didn't know where or what I wanted to be. Time was marching on. My bar mitzvah was fast approaching. Soon I would be a man. Then everything would be clear.

With my parents, the business of my grades was different. I couldn't wait to tell them, even if what they'd have to say was more or less the same thing they said after I came home with each report card.

My father: "Way to go, son," peering over my shoulder as he stood behind me poring over all the As before giving my hair a quick tousle and slipping away to another room in the house—probably the workshop, although anywhere would do—until dinner was ready.

My mother: "Of course you did. I knew you would," hijacking all of my As in the service of her greater achievement—her ability to know of my success beforehand.

Jerks, both of them. I wouldn't let them usurp my success

this time. At least not my mother. Not this year. It was a difficult year. Hairs were starting to sprout under my arms and between my legs, and I was having strange thoughts, about boys and men in general, and about Donny in particular. I sat myself down at the kitchen table while she was preparing dinner and made her suffer through the details of my mastery of all the subjects listed on my report card: Reading, History, Geography, Arithmetic, Social Studies and English. I read the "Comments" section aloud.

"Henry is a model student. He exhibits a sound knowledge of the subject and is eager to contribute to the classroom discussions." "Henry completes all assignments punctually. His handwriting is neat and his spelling and grammar are excellent." "Henry is without a doubt the smartest boy in the class, but he's not a show-off." "Henry is a joy to have in my class." "You should be proud of your son."

"It doesn't surprise me at all," my mother said as she chopped the iceberg lettuce.

"Mom?"

She stopped her chopping. "What is it?"

"Are you proud of me?"

"Of course I am. Why would you even ask such a thing?"

"Because you didn't tell me."

"Why should I have to tell you? Of course I am."

The tunnel behind the sofa was tempting, but the time wasn't ripe.

MY SHORT-LIVED CLAIM to fame in coolness was my transistor radio. "Radios are prohibited at school," the principal said during a special assembly. "They distract from more serious matters, and I will not tolerate such music infiltrating this establishment." What a jerk. He even wore a bowtie every day. I bought a transistor with my weekly allowance that I stuffed into a Band-Aid box hidden at the back of my underwear drawer. I counted the one- and five-dollar bills until they added up to the seventeen dollars I needed to buy one at Radio Shack, which was close enough to the house that I didn't need to ask my parents to drive me there and have to deal with an interrogation that would begin with "What do you need at Radio Shack?" and proceed until I was ensnared in a series of my own white lies and would have to confess.

The day after my furtive purchase, my mother went shopping in the late afternoon; my father was still at work. I extracted the thickest of my old fifth-grade textbooks from the bookshelf in my bedroom and took it to my father's workshop in the basement. Unlike the light-flooded dead zone of the living room, the below-ground workshop was a much-used room. My father spent most of his free time there. He didn't invite me in, and I rarely ventured in on my own. I couldn't even find where the wall switch was to turn on the overhead fluorescents. The tools and assorted jars and cans of screws, nails, wing nuts and other foreign objects on display suggested an impenetrable language or ritual that I had no interest in—like Chinese or football. But my father's workshop was the place where I stood a chance of contriving a way to carve a rectangular hollow into the 196 pages of the textbook, insert the radio, close the textbook cover, and take the genius contraption to school with me.

I chose a sharp implement hanging from a hook on one of the pegboard walls. I decided it was an awl. I couldn't say for sure, but the word sounded manly and technical and I wanted to use it to prove something to myself. I opened the front cover and the first twenty pages of the textbook and started stabbing and twisting through the remaining pages with the awl until I was able to yank out a rectangular chunk of paper that left a hole large enough for the radio. It was a sloppy job, but the radio fit snugly inside. I gathered up the paper shavings and stuffed them into my pockets.

The rest would be a breeze: slender earplug wire exposed

only along the back of my neck as it ran from the book through the sleeve of my shirt and collar and up to my ear. No one would notice. The recess bell would ring. Everyone would decamp to the playground, where I'd unplug the earbuds, turn the volume up and wait for the other kids to gravitate toward the source of the music: me. So cool. I polished the pennies in my loafers the night before and laid out the varsity blue cable-knit sweater vest with matching wool socks. My favorite outfit.

"You're listening to WIGB w-i-t-h... Corey ...DONOVAN!" Everyone's favorite DJ. Super handsome, from what I could tell by the headshot of him that Janet showed me at school the day after she'd taken a tour of the radio station while he was on the air. And his voice when he announced the songs. That voice was what cracked open the doors of another impenetrable language—my erotic fantasies. Donny was able to open that door too. All he had to do was pass by me in the hallway.

When the recess bell rang at 10:30, I made my way outside and positioned myself in an empty zone of the tarmac playground, watching everyone else being busy with someone along the edges of the cyclone fence, where clusters of pine trees offered a canopy for the secret goings-on of cliques. I turned on the transistor. Corey Donovan came through hugely in that first minute. "Here she is. Petula Clark and 'Downtown!'" Miss Lennon was nowhere in sight. I unplugged my earphone and ramped up the volume.

"*When you're alone and life is making you lonely...*" The students moved toward me, forming loose concentric bands around me. The cool ones, the popular ones, the most inaccessible ones, pushed their way closest. I thumbed the volume dial to full blast. "*You can always go...downtown,*" they sang aloud. Donny broke through the crowd and stood by my side. He put an arm around my shoulder and nudged me into a swaying position perfectly aligned with his. "*Maybe you know some little places to go...*" I fit well against him. We swayed well together. I felt us melting into each other. It scared me.

The shrill whistle sounded, the one that Miss Lennon kept around her neck and used too frequently to provoke fear, although it did stop us in our tracks. She'd appeared out of nowhere. "That's enough!" she shouted. I turned off the radio and snapped the book cover shut. "What's all this business? Disperse!"

Everyone slinked away except Donny. "That was the best," he said.

"Corey Donovan is the best. I bet if I asked my mom, she'd drive us over to WIGB for a tour and we can meet him."

He turned his face to mine. "Are you for real?"

I waited for him to hold me tighter, bring his face closer, so that I could smell his breath. He didn't do these things. "He's there on Tuesdays. Tomorrow. I'll ask my mom to take us after school."

"That would be amazing." He still didn't do the things I was waiting for him to do, but he did sit next to me on the school bus that afternoon. The ride was bumpy and his upper arm rubbed against mine often enough to make me be able to pretend he did it on purpose.

He raised his arm to point out the window. "Check out the Robinsons' driveway," he said as we were approaching his house. "We're in luck. Looks like a refrigerator box." Discarded boxes from newly acquired large appliances were prized treasures among the kids in the neighborhood, and refrigerator boxes were the best. They were tall enough that we didn't have to stoop inside once we'd transformed one into a secret clubhouse. After we dragged a large box to a secluded spot in one of our back yards, everyone took a turn writing a warning on its outer walls: "Keep out!" "No trespassing!" "Enter at your own risk!" "Members only!" Rules were established, officials elected, adventures imagined. Nothing happened in the clubhouse. It was about the preparation—the eligibility requirements, the regulations. Once these had been established, interest withered, and the box sat unused until it bloated from dewy mornings and collapsed into a soggy mass.

"Let's drag it to my house," he said. "We'll stick it under the maple tree by the log pile."

"Let's leave it. I wanna get home and ask my mom about tomorrow."

"Too cool," he said. He slapped my back. That's the thing he did to me. I was hoping for a gentler contact, something that would reveal his long-brewing affection for me and his desire for romance, even if it would have to be kept secret. The slap was a clumsy offering, and it hurt. Not romantic at all. Still. Maybe that was his way. At least for now. If that was the case, then it was a pain I'd suffer.

I asked my mother if she'd take us. "We'll see," she said. "Donald is such a nice boy."

"He sure is. So you'll take us?"

"We'll see."

She was hoping I'd forget about it by the next day. "We'll see? See what?" I asked. "Can't you just take us? I already told him you would."

"Now why did you go and do a thing like that?"

"Because I really want to go. So does he. He's such a great guy."

"I know you want to go. And I know he's a good boy, but right now I need to get dinner started."

"And if you take us, you'll stay in the car and wait for us, right? It won't take long."

"What am I supposed to do in the car?"

"Wait for us."

"I don't see why I can't..."

"Mom. Please. We won't be long."

"We'll see."

She headed toward the kitchen. I went to my bedroom, closed the door and dropped onto my bed. A nice boy. A good boy. She'd said it herself. Tomorrow after school, I'd find myself in the soundproof room of a radio station with Corey Donovan and Donny. Beyond cool, I kept repeating to myself inside as my body caught fire and my right hand snaked through the buttoned lip of my pants and the band of my underpants. Another secret place, but one that I visited often. The space between my shoulder blades still smarted from the smack Donny gave me. I reminded myself that maybe it was his weird way of letting me know how much I meant to him. Way better than no touch at all.

"SORRY HONEY," MY mother said when I came home from school the next day. "I'll have to take you another time. I called to make an appointment with Delores this morning and she only had one slot left. In an hour."

"Mom, your hair looks fine."

"The gray roots and the split ends are driving me crazy."

Roots? Split ends? What was she talking about? Her hair always looked the same.

"But Mom."

"I'll take you another time."

"What'll I tell Donny?" I corrected myself. "I mean Donald. He was counting on it."

"Tell him what I just told you: Another time."

"If there is another time." Making her suffer was in order. I stormed out of the kitchen toward the living room sofa and sat on the long side, the side reserved for my mother and Aunt Leah at Thanksgiving. My head didn't extend far enough above the sofa back to be able to rest against the wall, so I brought my knees up to my chest and let the grimy soles of my Keds push into the sofa cushion. Something needed to get soiled before I crawled behind the sofa to set up house. I had it all worked out. When my mother left for her stupid hair appointment, I'd call Donny and tell him to come over. I'd rummage through the kitchen and stock up on supplies—

the jar of peanut butter, the box of Ritz crackers, the carton of milk, the package of bologna, some Wonder Bread, and the bag of marshmallows. Then I'd head to my bedroom and grab the two pillows on my bed and the transistor radio on my chest of drawers. I'd shove everything to the far end of the tunnel. Donny would knock at the front door. Hopefully he'd be wearing his short, baggy soccer shorts and sleeveless jersey. I'd let him in and lead him directly to the sofa. "Let's go back here," I'd say. "Cool," he'd say, and he'd smack me on the shoulder. I'd let him go first so that I could watch his every movement from up close and behind, accidentally brushing against him from time to time on the way in. When we were positioned comfortably in the tight space, I'd tell him the news: "She's not going to take us." I'd look for signs of disappointment, even sadness, on his face. The more sadness I could make out, the better chance I'd have of persuading him to move in with me here. Forever. I'd show him the food supplies, the two pillows, the transistor. "It'll be great," I'd say. He'd look directly into my eyes and then he'd...

"Here you go, sweetheart." My mother came into the living room carrying a plate of Oreos arranged in a semicircle like fallen dominoes. "A special snack for you."

If only I could refuse her, but here we were, Mom and me, using the unused living room, and she didn't tell me to put my feet down or to not make a mess. She simply rubbed the back of her left hand along my shoulder, the way I imagined Donny touching me once we'd settled in behind the sofa to live there. She smiled into my eyes, turned around and walked away. "See you when I get back." She'd gotten the better of me. She usually did. She knew things about me beforehand.

"Okay, Mom." I took an Oreo and twisted it until it opened and I could scrape off the white filling with my teeth. It felt cool against my top incisors, the way fingertips feel when they're pressed against a windowpane on a crisp autumn morning. I took another. And another. When I finished the last Oreo, I looked at my watch. An hour had gone by. Donny hadn't shown up or called me, which meant he wouldn't. How could he have forgotten about WIGB? As I brushed the cookie crumbs off my lap onto the carpeting, I pictured him feeling up some girl in his rec room. He probably did things like that whenever he could. He bragged about it enough. How foolish I was. How stupid could I be to think that someone like him could want someone like me? Even so, I couldn't shake him.

The following day, I waited until Donny and I got off the school bus and were walking the rest of the way home before I said, "Sorry about yesterday."

"Yesterday?"

"The tour. WIGB and Corey Donovan. My mom was going to take us there after school."

"Oh. Right. I forgot," he said. I wanted to punch his face into a reaction. My phys. ed. teacher once called my overhand pitch "girly" in front of everyone. God only knew how my punch would be. I held back and dug my hand into my school bag instead.

"Let's see if the refrigerator box is still there," he said. "It'll probably be. Garbage day isn't until tomorrow."

I rifled through my school bag. I needed time to figure out what, if anything, to say. There were many possibilities to consider, from a simple "Okay" to "Maybe later" to "Go to hell." I remained silent while I considered and dismissed each possibility.

"What's up with you?" He asked the question I was hoping he'd ask, even if there was no way I'd be able to respond. There was too much I wanted to tell him, but I couldn't find a beginning, a middle or an end. Words and phrases floated that didn't join together right: gym shorts; soundproof studio; confessions; connection; touching. Love. I kept fiddling with my schoolbag and saying nothing. Maybe he'd go on to answer the question he asked me. He did.

"I get it," he said with a smirk that I'd seen only when he

was talking to girls. "Gotta be love. You're in love, right? Who is it?"

I stopped my fiddling, gathered my bearings and looked him directly in the eye. "You tell me. Who do you think I'm in love with?"

He reached over and tweaked my nipple, which hurt more than when he'd slapped my back. "I bet it's Cindy. The girl in Geography with the big boobs. They're real. She doesn't stuff her bra."

"How do you know?"

"Chet told me. He copped a feel under the bleachers."

I'd never considered big boobs as a factor for anything, let alone love.

"Fess up," he said. "You're into her."

"Fuck off."

We arrived at his driveway. "Catch you tomorrow. You're smitten. I can tell." He tweaked my other nipple, harder than usual, and walked away toward his house.

I watched him close the front door behind him and seal me off from the life he lived when he wasn't with me. I continued down the sidewalk, past all the houses and lawns I'd seen hundreds of times. This was my zone, my world. Suddenly it seemed small, smaller than a refrigerator box or a tunnel behind a sofa. I couldn't wait to outgrow it, venture beyond, to a place that didn't make me feel out of place. There had to be one. I wondered whether Donny thought about these things too and, if he did, whether he'd let me know so we could end up understanding each other in important ways and explore together. Forever. Another foolish thought, so stupid, but I couldn't shake it. I couldn't imagine it not ending up that way. My nipple smarted.

My mother's car wasn't in the driveway when I got home.

"Mom?" I wasn't expecting a response. Still, at that hour of the day, the empty house unsettled me. My mother was like a much-used room, if only to escape from to some other space—my bedroom, the rec room or, one day, the sofa tunnel. Without her buzzing about, the house felt vast and aimless, without purpose. If only Donny had shown up yesterday. The two of us could have redefined space, starting with the sofa tunnel. I missed the friction of him. My mother was probably running an errand, but I missed her too. I didn't understand what it was I missed about her exactly. I figured it had to do with the way she didn't get all worked up about whatever version of myself I happened to be trying out in front of her to see if it was a good fit, even the one about being adopted.

$$Two$$

Your mother doesn't know from slums," my father said when she got lost in her stories of deprivation. "Where she lived, they had stores. Where I lived, we had scrap heaps." My father was born in Philadelphia too, but in the southern part of the city limits, where the tallest buildings were the oil refineries. "It stunk like chemicals everywhere. In the air, my clothes, my hair. You got used to the smell. Like when you have a steady case of the farts." In his neck of the woods, so he said, there were no shops at ground level, just endless rows of one-story housing units slapped together for the families of the men who worked in the refineries. The wives didn't plant flowers in pots and didn't have aluminum awnings. To do their shopping, they had to take the trolley elsewhere, to better ghettos, like the one where my mother lived, where you could not only find plums but you could buy a bushel basket of them for a song.

"I spent my free time playing in the scrap yards with my friends. We scavenged for bottle caps. There were plenty of them in the mountains of junk. You had to get past the stench of everything else while you were rooting around for them. We flipped them. I don't remember how the game worked, but those bottle caps were as precious as gold coins. They meant everything to us." He smiled when he mentioned the bottle caps. He'd told me the bottle-cap story many times. If it weren't for the smile that gave character to his otherwise bland face whenever he told it, I would have been bored.

"My best friend was the bottle-cap champion. He could root them out like nobody. Donald. That's your friend's name, isn't it?" he reminded me numerous times, as if that shared first name was enough to establish a strong father–son connection. "Yep. Donald. Goldfarb. Yours?"

"Armstrong. Donald Armstrong."

"Right. Sounds Irish." The way he said "Irish" made me understand that he wasn't paying a compliment to Donny. His eyebrows and lips dipped down, the way they do when there's disapproval.

"He's a good student. And he's on the football team."

"Good for him. Luck o' the Irish. Let's see how he ends up."

ADRIENNE WAS BORN in Philadelphia too, in a city hospital several blocks from the neighborhood our parents moved to once my father's salary could allow it. That neighborhood—the one before the neighborhood I remember growing up in—was part of the first concentric ring of new homes outside the inner-city part. "A real step up," my mother told me. "The row homes were well-kept. The neighbors had power mowers for their front lawns, and garages to keep them in. Mr. Davis used to wake your sister up on Sunday mornings when he mowed his grass next door. Never married," she said as her eyes glazed over and I could tell she was no longer talking to me. "I think he liked men. I saw men go into his house on nights when I couldn't sleep and I sat by the kitchen window trying to calm my nerves. That's how they do it. They sneak them in when they think no one is watching." Then she remembered she was talking to me. "You remember Mr. Davis, don't you? Nice yard. Strange man."

I remembered Mr. Davis and how in summer he mowed

his lawn bare-chested and I looked for excuses to knock on his door when he was done and hoped he'd ask me into his house. One time he saw me watching him. He turned off his mower and stood there, watching me back. The silence that traveled between him and me scared me. I turned away and wondered whether he was still looking at me. It was then that I felt the stirrings of something in common between this man and me that we'd never be able to reveal to each other. I was five or so. Yes, I remembered Mr. Davis.

"No, I don't remember him."

"A good neighbor. A strange man, though. A *feygele*." She fluttered her hands like baby wings. I tightened my wrists.

My mother showed me photos of the house. "We took a corner unit," she said. "It had windows on the sides, not only on the front and the back. You can't see them in the picture that well, but we had them on the sides. Such a difference it made. No more of the railroad apartments I was so used to." The photos she laid out were of small, low-ceilinged rooms burdened with thick, dark furniture handed down from dead relatives I'd never met. A few photos showed the small side windows she took such pride in. They gave onto a view of other small side windows across the narrow breezeway. She didn't find any photos of me. "Your hair was so blond then. Oy, such an angel you were, Henry. An angel! My little messiah."

She didn't call me those things when we'd upgraded to the suburban neighborhood composed of three- and four-bedroom split-level houses stamped out on one-acre lots. Each house was set at a different angle to offset the cookie-cutter effect. Whatever indigenous trees and shrubs were there before construction began had been yanked out by their roots to make way for cement and asphalt—foundations, driveways, sidewalks, walkways leading to side and back doors—and the zoysia grass inseminated on each lawn. Some of the lots were left in their original hilly condition, others were leveled to flatness by large trucks with fang-like appendages attached to their hoods and big men maneuvering the appendages with an assortment of stick shifts that had different colored knobs on top of them. I remember those trucks and the men in them, watching them as they labored and sweated in other yards, since my parents decided not to level the hills on our lot. I remember that the last strands of my blond hair had already darkened to red. This house was the one I grew up in, the one my heart and soul belonged to, especially in winter.

Our yard had the best hills. Their gradations of slope treachery brought every kid in the neighborhood to our place, sled tucked under one arm. That's how I met Donny. He arrived at our driveway with his Flexible Flyer and was wearing a wooly cap that stretched below his ears and eyebrows. His nose was red from the cold and his cheeks were flushed. His lips were red too, but that could be their natural color. He was probably older than me. He was taller, his shoulders broader, his feet larger. I kept my distance but couldn't take my eyes off him, except when I feared he might notice me gawking.

At school the next day, he tapped me on the shoulder from behind. I turned around.

"Hey," he said. His face seemed familiar, but all that red hair threw me off. I stared at him and said nothing.

"It's me. Donny."

"Hey." I still didn't recognize him.

"Your yard is something. That last curve before you hit the street is a killer. I almost flipped over. Did you see?"

I recognized the voice. It was the one I'd imagined the boy in my yard having—deep, masculine, self-assured—as I watched his every movement on the hills the day before I knew who he was. He was that boy.

"I'll be back for sure."

"Sure," I said. I pushed out two more words. "Any time."

He did come back to my yard with his sled. The second time he came, he pulled a bar of soap from his coat pocket.

"Here. Use this," he said.

My gloved hand met his gloved hand to take the soap. "Where? For what?"

He removed his gloves. "Rub it along the blades like this," he instructed me, moving his exposed hand up and down in the air as if he were stroking the length of a goose's neck. "It makes the sled go faster."

I removed my gloves, did as he told me, and handed him the soap back. My naked hand met his and for a split second I felt warm.

"Come," he said. "Leave your sled here and follow me."

He pulled his Flexible Flyer up the steepest hill until we reached the top. I trailed behind him. God forbid I was close enough to actually have to talk about something.

He pointed his sled toward where we came from and lay belly-down on it, arms at his side like a torpedo. "Sit on top of me," he said. "Put your feet on the wings. You steer. I'll keep things balanced."

"Where should I sit?"

"Wherever. Try above my butt."

I did as he told me, straddling the sled and squatting down until my butt made contact with his lower back. As I placed my feet on the wings of his sled, I felt the weight of my body sink perfectly into the contours of his.

That's how I met Donny.

Those winter months of happiness went by quickly. Most intervals of happiness do. The snow lost its staying power in March. Donny disappeared too. Party over. When I complained about not having anything to do and not having anyone to do it with, my mother would say, "Go play in traffic." My father would take me by the arm, lead me out the back door and push me into the yard, fanning his arms like a proud peacock. "Look at all this," he'd say. "Now get out there and find something to do. There's plenty."

I looked around. I saw a bunch of bare trees and soggy

grass. They were indifferent to me. I looked at my father. He seemed indifferent to me too. "Such as?"

"*Boychik*, this is as close to a country club as we'll get that's not for *goyim* only." We had two country clubs in our suburb: Green Valley and Maple Glen.

"Yeah. Mom said the same thing. How do you know that?" I asked. "Is there a sign at the entrance or something?"

"As if they need to put up a sign. They have their ways."

I didn't know what he meant and didn't ask him. Most of the time his explanations didn't help me know something better. I didn't mind. I expected him to know a lot more than I did. It was his responsibility as a father. I relied on him to know everything and to keep me safe from what I didn't know. His job was to be right, and my job was to trust him, even when I understood little of what he was telling me and only felt the need to retain what he told me for eventual use, in the way my father stored used nails, molly bolts, nuts and screws in jars on the shelves of the garage/workshop. He was arming me for the future, creating solutions to problems that didn't yet exist, at the expense of helping me decipher my present. If he only understood how the simple glide of his hand along my cheek or through my hair, the tickle of his lips and mustache along the top of my head, would have helped. But that was soft work. Woman's work. He had more important things to do. Man things. Things I didn't understand and suspected I might never understand. Like the way Donny navigated the sharp curve near the street without a scratch. I was missing those kinds of genes. Such a curse.

I HAD MY own bedroom at the end of the hallway. My parents let me keep my door shut whenever I wanted to. Sometimes I thought it was because they trusted me; other times I thought they were plain indifferent to what I might be doing in there as long as I was out of the way. The bedroom hallway was long and dimly lit. At night, it seemed endless. When I was younger, my mother accompanied me to my bedroom and settled me in by reading to me. She hardly gave me enough time to look at the illustrations. "That's enough for tonight," she'd say after a page or two, as if she'd set a timer to go off to remind her that soothing a child's fear deserved no more than a blip of her precious time. She'd rise from my bed and switch off the light to leave me alone in the darkness.

"Mom, can you read me some more?" Most of the time she repeated, "That's enough for tonight. Now get some sleep," and proceeded in haste toward my bedroom door without looking back at me. Every once in a while she'd slow down, turn toward my bed and walk back to me, sinking onto the mattress as if my plea had registered as a legitimate need. She'd survey my airplane wallpaper without saying a word and then, turning toward me without looking at me, start talking about her childhood until she snapped back and said, "That's enough for tonight. I'm serious this time. Now go to sleep!" What she told me when she returned to me felt private, even if it didn't amount to much: a random tale or two from the days when she was my age, and sometimes a third tale if she wasn't ready to find her way back to her present life and all its travails. I enjoyed her Philly stories. They created images in my head that breathed life into the black and white snapshots in the family albums that lined the bottom cabinet of the hutch. But she spoke without looking at me, which made me believe that she wasn't really talking to me at all, that she was talking to herself out loud for her own benefit, not mine, and that the intimacy was between her and herself. Then it wasn't so comforting. Even so, on those rare nights when she came back to me and positioned herself on the corner of my mattress like a postage stamp licked securely onto an envelope, I fell asleep quickly.

When she was too busy or irritable to take me to my room, I asked my father to come with me. He pretended not to hear me.

"Dad? Please?"

"Listen, son…"

"Please?"

My father followed me down the hallway from behind; his footsteps were heavy and held a steady rhythm, like someone in a chain gang.

"There you go." He stopped short of the bedroom itself, positioning himself directly under the doorframe, half in and half out. It was up to me to say something that would lure him inside, show him I hung on his every word.

One time I said, "This country club business. No Jews? Is that a Philly thing?"

He crossed the threshold and walked toward the bed. My father and me in my bedroom at night. "I wish it were that simple," he said. "If it was just a Philly thing, we wouldn't have stayed here. We'd be someplace else. Probably Flushing Meadows, where your Aunt Esther lives. We used to go there a lot. Remember? We stayed there when we went to the World's Fair in the mid Sixties. We went to the fair for two days, but we stayed at your Aunt Esther's for two weeks. It was a test. We weren't thrilled with Flushing Meadows, though. Too crowded, like the old days."

"I had fun there. Her neighbor had lots of fun board games."

"We thought about Jerusalem too. I've never been there."

"You mean Jerusalem, Israel?"

"Yep. We'll get there one day." He sat on the bed and looked me in the eye. "It's not that simple, Henry. We don't belong, except for a few places. Small places, like Flushing Meadows and Jerusalem. You'll see one day."

As he spoke, my eyes focused on the strands of hair that curved around his wrist. They were dense and dark, tapering off as they rounded the pale underside. I rubbed my hand up and down my left wrist. It was as smooth as the soup bones my mother added to her stocks and stews. How I hated those bones and the gluey marrow in their centers. I didn't understand why she didn't remove them before she put the tureen and ladle in the center of the table. They got in the way of my utensils. When my father abandoned his utensils and picked up the bones with his fingers to suck the marrow, images came to mind of terms I'd learned in Science class: Cro-Magnon man, Neanderthal man, Pithecanthropus erectus. I was sure my father's wrists were like theirs, primitive and essential. Mine were hairless and weak. He sucked marrow out of bones.

"You'll see," my father repeated.

"When?" I asked. When would I be old enough to have an understanding of the whole of everything? I inspected my wrists and lower arms every day for signs of hair and the assurance it would bring. I wondered what my father's wrists smelled like. I didn't know much about anything.

He rose from my bed, walked toward the door, and closed it behind him. Conversation over. "What does he know about anything anyway?" I asked myself. The question helped a little, but I wish he'd stayed with me a little longer, if only because Donny's father played golf at one of those country clubs and I wanted to understand that. My father would have had something to say.

ON RAINY DAYS, I wasn't allowed to play outside, which made no sense to me. I didn't have any problem putting on my olive slicker and black galoshes to fight the elements. It felt like trying on a new person, someone I might be happy with. I didn't mind if it meant getting soaked. My mother did.

"Are you crazy?" she asked. "You'll track mud in the house and catch cold. That's all I need now."

It wasn't worth arguing about, especially when she said things like that, which made my mere existence amount to an annoyance. I hung my rain slicker back on the hook by the front door. "Ooookaaay, Mom."

Outdoors, Donny and I roamed like stray dogs through neighbors' backyards, along the quiet streets and cul-de-sacs of the neighborhood and, if we'd lost all sense of time and constraint, into the woods across the main street that marked the end of our neighborhood and the beginning of another world, where we once found a fist-size skull; another time a mattress with blood stains on it; another time a bullet casing that coated my fingers with gray dust when I touched it. Outdoors we sweated, our legs ached, and we stopped only when we came upon an unexpected find or when we had to catch our breath along the way. He made me want to break rules. With him I was willing to, convinced that an act of daring on my part would be handsomely rewarded. It would transport us to a moment when he felt safe enough to reveal the unthinkable to me: that he was in love with me. That's the way love happened. My mother's book covers insisted on it. They were scattered throughout the house, romance novels, with photos of a man, a woman, wind-blown hair, an air of great suffering, and words in their titles like "Tempest," "Storms," "Passion" and "Transport."

I sensed it was about to happen once when we were sitting on a fallen trunk of an oak tree in the woods and not saying anything. With him, silence didn't make me nervous. I didn't need to break it. He didn't seem to, either. The quiet between us was its own language, our language, a code of intimacy that only we understood.

This time, he was the one to break it. Someone had to. It couldn't go on forever. "Give me your hand," he said. I extended it. He took it gently in his and brought it directly above the zipper area of his shorts. "Do you trust me?" he asked. I did, but I let my half of the silence continue. He'd intuit it meant that I trusted him. He curled my fingers into the palm of my hand and then extended my index finger until it pointed toward the sky while he pulled his penknife from his pocket with his free hand. I imagined him carving a clean line deep into my wrist before proceeding to do the same to his. In that place and moment, I would have let him.

"You can close your eyes if you want." I didn't. He made a nick on the tip of my extended finger and waited until a drop of blood gathered. "Hold your finger up," he said as he did the same to his index finger. Then he rubbed his finger against mine until our two red pearls of blood merged. "There," he said. "Now we're blood brothers."

What to do with my hand? If I let it drop naturally, it would land on his groin. If I pulled it toward me, it would signify game over. I didn't want the game to end that way. I didn't want the game to end at all. I sat there, paralyzed and mute, waiting for his next move.

"Agreed?"

I turned my head from our joined fingers to his eyes, hoping that his were already waiting to meet mine. It was hard to tell. The trees cast long shadows in the waning sunlight. "Brothers?"

"That's what you call it when you do this." He withdrew his finger from mine and guided my hand back to me. When he let go, I felt banished from him, without any possibility of my bringing my hand back close to him as a dare to him, to us, to go further. I looked at the flattened red blotches on the tips of our index fingers that our blended drops of blood had created. His was elongated, mine was wider. The color was the same deep red. He stood up and brushed the bits of bark off the seat of his pants. Then he wiped his bloodied finger onto his back pocket. It would probably leave a stain. "I have to be home soon. Let's get moving."

"Where to next?"

He shook his head. "Home. Where else?" I didn't understand. Was he annoyed with me for my stupid question? Was he annoyed at himself for having chosen me as his partner in the blood ritual? He ran in place for a few seconds to rev up. Beads of sweat from the tips of his hair sprayed around him like a fragmented halo. None of them landed on me.

"Go ahead. I'll hang back."

"Okay," he said. "Later." I watched him as he darted like some form of wildlife through low-lying branches and over uneven ground surfaces until his physical presence dwindled to a possibility of insignificance. His red hair was the last visible sign of him I could make out before he disappeared altogether where the woods met the main street and the world that I inhabited, the world that wasn't enough.

It rained the day after Donny and I became blood brothers. I was confined to the house and my own company. My mother was home, but I didn't expect her to entertain me and had no desire for her to. I heard her Mixmaster start to whir in the kitchen and headed to my parents' bedroom, the most unfamiliar room of the house. Frills and fabrics accentuated the room, from the blue and white paisley valences above the windows to the matching sham pillows on the bed, and further down to the pleated dust-ruffle that brushed against the deeper-blue pile carpeting that was flecked with white. The white flecks in the carpet were meant to be part of the décor, but they were indistinguishable from the lint and dust that needed to be vacuumed. The color-coordinated plushness was so insistent that I was sure it had to be a cover for something harder, messier, more violent—what with all those gothic romances of hers lying about the house. Then there was the centerpiece of the room: the king-size bed whose four thick posts rose like brazen totems that tapered toward the top until they mushroomed at the tip. My parents slept together, and some nights I heard sounds coming from them that definitely weren't words. Strange sounds, animal sounds, a confusion of pain and pleasure. I couldn't distinguish between the two when I heard those sounds in their room at night. I knew that they had to have sex in that bed and wondered if something about the sex they did was responsible for such sounds. I wondered what was missing in me that kept me from feeling sex—

at least in the way I'd heard about it—as an act so pressing and all-important.

Night after night, the noises I heard them make convinced me that their bedroom had to be hiding objects, in drawers or under the mattress, that would reveal messy secrets about their life when they weren't so busy working and cleaning and cooking and taking care of me and my sister. If only I could find one secret between them, to assure me that my own turbulences were okay, that adults had them too.

The walls of their room were painted taupe. It was the name of a color I discovered from previous riflings in their room when I found an unopened package of pantyhose in my mother's chest of drawers. The adhesive label on the plastic said "taupe." I'd never heard the word before and wasn't even sure how to pronounce it. Tope? Tawp? It sounded exotic, all the more so because how was I supposed to know my mother wore pantyhose? My parents didn't go out much at night. Another time I found a small cobalt-blue metal toolbox in my father's night table. I muttered "Darn" when I saw the tiny keyhole under the release button and assumed the box was locked. I put it away quickly, without pushing the button to see if the lid would snap open.

On this rainy indoor day, however, my mother had just turned on the Mixmaster. There was time to take my time. I extracted the box from my father's night table drawer, placed it on his side of the bed and pressed the button. The lid snapped open. Envelopes and loose papers were piled inside. How boring. As I closed the lid, the edge of one sheet of paper stuck out of the left lip of the box. I opened the lid again and tried to compress the stack so the wayward edge would sink down. It was too thick. I pulled the sheet out from among the other thinner papers. A birth certificate. My name appeared on the top line in a serious calligraphy, like musical notations or the Declaration of Independence; in the right margin were miniature footprints, whose venations were as intricate and one-of-a-kind as a snowflake or a Chinese engraving. My mother's Mixmaster stopped whirring as I was finishing reading "Overland Park, Kansas" on the "Place of Birth" line. Kansas? I stuffed the certificate back into the box, closed the lid, and shoved the box back into the drawer.

Two days later, when I heard my mother vacuuming on the ground floor, I scurried to their room, to the box, took out the certificate and tucked it under my T-shirt. I dug deeper through the papers in the box until I felt another box inside that I'd brushed against before. I opened it and extracted the top layer of nine aluminum packets, whose three rows and three columns were fastened into a panel with perforations. I folded the columns accordion-like into one long, thick strip and put the nine condoms into my pocket.

Later that day I pulled them out of my pocket and dangled them in front of my mother while she was chopping a head of iceberg lettuce. I asked her what they were even though I knew what they were. She released the knife and the head of lettuce. They landed on the chopping board.

"Where did you get those?" she asked.

"What are they?" I asked.

Donny had already bragged to me about how much he knew about condoms. "Slip them on your manhood and you're ready to pump away," he said. "It doesn't feel as good as the real thing, but who wants to deal with having a baby?" The image of pumping away made me cringe, but I had to stay the course. His course. "No kidding," I said. I didn't believe that he'd actually done what he'd described, and he probably didn't believe I had either. But we had our dance, and I followed his lead, hoping it would bring us so close that he would find a way to love me back. I struggled to believe that the stigma of our red hair gave us a special affinity even though I was convinced that he and I hung out simply because we lived in the same neighborhood and were about the same age. Nothing more. I just happened to love him, and the risk of him abandoning me, even over one badly chosen word or gesture, was always there.

With my mother, I could tread pretty much as I pleased. I might need to be extra sweet in order to earn a second scoop of ice cream, but not to earn her love. We were too joined. I'd lived inside her body until I was too big to fit. Once she'd managed to push me outside of her, I was still her, and she still me. It couldn't be otherwise, which gave me the luxury of being able to provoke her without risk as I tried to fit some-where outside of her, which was taking a helluva long time. At worst, she could seethe with exasperation, throw her hands in the air and tell me to go play in traffic. But she could never let me go. Unless I was adopted. Better to keep the birth certifi-cate under my T-shirt—Kansas?—and grill her about the con-doms instead.

Mom wiped her hands on her apron. "Balloons." She con-tinued wiping them. "Yes, balloons. You know, for special occa-sions. Your birthday, for example. It's coming up, you know."

"Yep."

She stopped wiping and resumed her chopping. "What do you want on top of your cake this year? In my day, we didn't put miniature trains or doll houses on top of cakes. We were lucky to have cake. But that was in my day."

"Your day? Which day was that?"

"Which day was what?"

"Mom, you just said 'In my day' twice. Which day?"

The evenly chopped lettuce covered the chopping board as if it was a manicured lawn. "You really are something. Sometimes I wonder where you came from."

She offered me a cucumber slice that was sitting in a side dish. As I reached over to take it, I said, "Beats me. Maybe I was adopted," while I worked my free hand toward the birth certificate.

"Henry," she said, "do me a favor. Get the tomatoes from the fridge. And the ranch dressing. I got the ranch this morn-ing. Just for you. It's on the door by the mayonnaise. The bot-tle that's shaped like a cello. It was on sale."

"I know, Ma."

"Know what?"

"I know where you keep the dressing. And I know which bottle it is."

"Anything else you want to tell me that you know?"

"I don't know. What else should I know?"

She pointed the paring knife at me and started brandishing it in the air like a magic wand or an épée. "Do me another favor. Go play in traffic. Make yourself scarce." I put the condoms back in my pocket and skipped off, relieved that we'd found our way back inside the safe borders of our sarcasm. I wasn't ready to cross over with the matter of the birth certificate. Overland Park, Kansas? Still, I couldn't decide whether I should put the condoms and the birth certificate back in their secret spot or find a secret spot of my own. I might need them one day, although I couldn't imagine when. Or why.

Three

Donny wasn't adopted. He didn't need to tell me. Looking at him, you could see right away and everywhere the imprint of his mom, but with lots of bits of his father: the bump on the top of the nose, the sliver of space between the upper front teeth, the downward-sloped shoulders that arched back when he walked, and the slightly bowed legs, which made me picture a heart, until I heard other boys call them cowboy legs. They weren't making fun of him. They envied his cowboy legs. I did too. I wondered if some of the other boys were in love with him.

When Donny told me that he asked his mom if he was adopted, I said, "Why did you ask her?"

"I was bored. She was getting on my nerves. I wanted to get on hers."

"What did she say?" She had to have said no. Still, I was curious to hear how she would have said it. Mrs. Armstrong was all about tenderness and comfort. Their house smelled like homemade baked goods, even in the bathroom. Our bathrooms smelled like Pine-Sol. I imagined her saying something like, "Of course not, my sweet silly boy," and then mussing up his hair to reassure him that she loved his red mop and everything else about him before she scooted him off to play with one of the games his parents bought him that my parents didn't buy me. I wondered sometimes whether I was drawn to Donny because of all the toys he had. Deep down I didn't believe that. We didn't spend much time indoors. Walls made him restless; his restlessness made me awkward. He was in his element outdoors, where he could breathe and I could trail him, hoping that his way of being a guy would spread to me; I also wanted to catch whiffs of him from behind.

"What do you think she said?" That's when he told me that she said no and hugged him too hard.

"Good for you."

"What's so good about it? I wanted to stir up a little trouble."

"Then you should've asked her something else, jerk," I said. I'd never called him a jerk before. I was terrified I'd gone too far.

"You never know," he said.

"C'mon. You knew. Or else you wouldn't have asked her."

"Who's being the jerk now?" he said. "What's the big deal?"

I got up to leave. "Why did you even bother asking her?" His face was tight and hard, as if all the water it contained (which was a lot, our science teacher had told us) had been sucked out of him and risen into the atmosphere where it would migrate at the whim of the wind and deposit itself elsewhere, far away. His upper lip, full and red like his hair, was reduced to a razor-thin line. I had to get away from him so badly that I turned down his offer to play Monopoly.

"C'mon. You can have the cannon this time," he said as I headed for the front door.

"That's okay." I opened the door and peered into the gray and damp outdoors. The rain had subsided to a drizzle-mist and the cloud formations were floating west, away from us. He would never love me, even if I let him have Marvin Gardens or Boardwalk.

"Who's being the jerk?" he called as I walked down the driveway between his mother's red Cutlass Supreme and his father's white Lincoln Continental. I envied families that had cars like that. Their achievements were so abundant inside the house that they must be spilled onto the driveway. My parents had matching Dodge Darts, one pewter and the other a lighter shade of gray that didn't have a special name that I was aware of. Drab. I sped up. Donny and his parents' dazzling cars vanished in the obscuring drizzle.

By the time I reached the bottom of the driveway, I was missing him. I shouldn't have walked out. He shouldn't have closed the front door after shouting at me. But that's what we did to each other. When I reached the street, I considered turning around to see if he'd opened his front door to look for me, in which case I would have come up with something to say to bring him back into my life. I could have told him about the blue box and my birth certificate with Overland Park, Kansas inscribed on the second line. I could have asked him what he thought about it, even though he'd have said something stupid. But I didn't turn around. It was getting darker. I didn't have a clue about what could tear us further apart or draw us closer together. I kept going. In the familiar path of darkness that took me from his house to mine, I tried to understand how someone could come to mean something as important as oxygen for someone else, and why Donny, of all people, was that for me. What did we have in common?

Tetherball. Our passion for it was equal, whatever the reason, if passion needs a reason. We spent most of the hours between when school let out and dinner was ready smacking the ball with open palms and watching how tightly the rope wound against the pole that Donny's dad had fixed into the earth like a phallic totem meant to withstand the ravages of time. We were in it for the shared effort and exhaustion, the delirious release of energies pounding away at our insides like dogs in a frenzy of heat. For me, our bouts of tetherball were a relief so exquisite that they had to be about intimacy, a state of wordlessness. I was convinced that Donny had to feel it too. Our tetherball sessions passed in the blink of an eye, even when they were entering their second hour and were made to come to an abrupt end when his mother called, "Dinner is ready!" and only then did we notice it was getting dark outside. Without that summons, we might have continued smacking the ball into the dead of night, when we couldn't see where the ball was going, in the same way that we hit the ball in total silence when we had so much we could have been saying. A second call: "Dinner is on the table!" How could it be so late so fast? We tallied the score. It made no difference to me who was winning. I waited for his hand to slap mine, regardless of who won. "Later," he'd say. I'd be left with a sweet stinging sensation on my hand from the slap, and a bit more of history with Donny accrued. I was content.

When we weren't playing tetherball, we didn't talk all that much either. We might have, if I'd had the courage. But I was too afraid of losing him by talking too much and letting slip impulses and unformed thoughts that might push him away. That's what a best friend was. Someone you knew you could confess to most and were afraid of losing most. Someone you knew you could talk to but were quiet with, hoping that they'd hear all the words that weren't being spoken. Donny made it so easy. When I nattered on too long, he had no qualms about saying to me, "Will you shut up already? Cripes!"

By the time I arrived at the Lehmanns' driveway, four driveways from his, the darkness had swallowed Donny's house and my ambivalence over not telling him about the birth certificate. I decided that I'd done the right thing. Donny was competitive. It was his trademark. He was used to winning, and his victories made me proud to be his friend—maybe his best friend, I prayed—even if I couldn't understand how or why he might possibly consider me to be the same thing for him. It couldn't be out of pity. Winners didn't sympathize with losers—they fed off them. I'd seen Donny bully enough scrawny guys to get that. He wasn't one to go all soft. I hated thinking about my best friend that way, but I couldn't help but think that way. That's who he was. What I didn't under-stand was whether he was my best friend because I knew him so well or because he remained a mystery despite how much I knew him. "Where and how did love come about?" I asked myself. "From the light or from the dark?" Then I reminded myself that I didn't get around to asking my mother if I was adopted.

The front door was unlocked when I arrived home. I went upstairs to my bedroom. Closing my bedroom door behind me, I decided that Donny shouldn't be my friend anymore, best or otherwise. He gave me pangs of hunger constantly. My resolve was short-lived. By the time I flopped on my bed, the prospect of not spending time with him again was unbearable. I couldn't imagine getting through my days without Donny's way of being, without the fragrance of him goading me to take in deep breaths of him.

AT HOME, WE washed with Irish Spring. The bars of marble-ized green and white were nestled on each soap dish embedded in the walls above the bathroom sinks and bathtubs. The soap left a long-lasting after-scent of industrial-strength disinfec-tant mixed with something earthy, loamy. My mother made me shower every other night. After school, when I boarded the school bus to go home, I had the habit of tilting my head toward my armpits to sniff for signs of B.O. Nothing. Even after gym class on warm days in September and June. I blamed it on Irish Spring's secret formula, but deep down I feared that my inability to produce B.O. was due to my not being man enough. Donny managed to exude his own smell even in the winter months when he didn't sweat at all. I wondered whether his red hair had something to do with it.

One afternoon I asked him whether he used Irish Spring.

"Irish string?" he replied. "What's that?"

"No, Irish Spring."

"Oh." He paused. "What's that?"

"You should know. You're Irish."

He repeated, "What is it?"

"Never mind. Forget it."

"Shower time, then off to bed with you," my mother called that night at eight o'clock sharp. The call was for me, not for Adrienne. My sister took at least two showers a day. Long ones. So long that my mother would trek to the bathroom door and holler, "Get out already, unless you want to pay the water bill!" Adrienne believed that cleanliness was crucial to get boys. I thought smelling fresh and fragrant kept them away.

"Okay, Ma." On shower night it didn't matter where in the house I was at eight o'clock or what I was doing. I didn't put up a fight or ask for an extension. I expected my mother to call out to me at that hour with those eight words, and she expected to hear my two-word reply. Both of us knew what it meant: the onset of evening was arriving, the interval when activities conducted in sharp light ceded to forces of the darkening sky. Daylight defined borders. Darkness blotted them out. The interval between was neither here nor there, perfect for the adoption question.

I imagined her starting to answer with "Well, dear..." followed by a few syllables of pause to collect her thoughts. I'd match her two-word ante and raise it by one: "Am I adopted?" It would be audacious on my part, and she'd put me in my place by saying something harsh to end the discussion then and there so she could get back to the other things she usually attended to at that hour—usually sitting with my father in the den to watch television while she clipped coupons from the newspaper. "Do me a favor," she'd say. "Go finish your homework. Such nonsense!"

I'd skulk to my bedroom, open a textbook and stare into space until I could hear her approaching my door. She'd rap gently. "Henry, dear. Come down and say good night to your father." She'd speak gently to pull me back into the light of her. She needed me as much as I needed her.

"Almost done. Be there in a minute."

She'd enter my room. "Sweetheart," she'd say, "You came to us" or "Our wish was granted in you" or "We knew right away that you were the one." Something disarmingly sweet and not her. I'd give her the meanest expression I was capable of contorting my soft facial features into to let her know that what she said didn't work, that she hadn't practiced it enough. I'd get up and leave my room, march down the hallway and stairs, and slam the back door behind me. I'd be sad and scared, but liberated from something that felt tight. I'd never come back. First stop, Donny's house.

That's what I imagined. But I didn't ask her at sunset that day. I hadn't practiced enough. I asked her at the breakfast table on the day after—a Saturday—when the sun was casting thick bars of light across the kitchen counter, the floor and the table. On Saturdays, everyone slept in and we didn't eat breakfast until late, sometimes as late as eleven o'clock.

"Breakfast is ready!" And we were ready too, my father, Adrienne and me. Our bedroom doors opened almost in unison and the three of us charged toward the breakfast table.

She'd laid out pancakes, bacon, a mixture of warmed syrup and butter in a ramekin dish, and a pitcher of orange juice that she'd prepared from a can of frozen concentrate. The pancakes were perfectly round. The ramekin dish glistened with golden orbs of melted butter floating on the top of the amber syrup. The paper napkins were folded into neat triangles. All was illuminated by the rays of the almost-afternoon sun streaming in through the bay window, as if each ray was tasked with gilding the elements of an exemplary domestic life. By the time I arrived, my father was already seated at the table, dressed in a polo shirt and madras pants. His round of golf at the Jewish alternative to a country club began at noon. He'd pile food onto his plate, eat quickly and say little. Adrienne was already there too, still in her pink empress-cut nightgown that was too transparent for the budding breasts it was revealing underneath. Perfect circles of pancakes, madras golf pants, teenage girl tits. A family breakfast on a weekend. How to upend all of it?

"How did you get the pancakes to be so fluffy this time, Mom?" Adrienne asked as I took my place next to her. The table was oval; us kids sat on one long side, the parents on the other. The curved ends were empty.

"A little extra baking powder, and I let the batter sit longer so it would rise more," she replied.

"How many strips of bacon can I take, Edith?" my father asked.

"Four apiece. You can have one of mine, if you want." They winked at each other. A dose of happiness over a bacon strip. The overdose.

"Mom, am I adopted?"

She took a fifth slice of bacon between the tongs and brought it toward my father. "Why would you ask such a thing?" She positioned the bacon on the side of my father's plate and released the tongs. She smiled at him and he smiled back. Happiness continued. "My sweet silly son."

"Am I?"

The way they were looking at each other made both of them laugh. "What on earth?" he said.

Adrienne joined in. "I bet it's Donny. I bet he put you up to it. He always makes you different than what we're used to you being."

"Hush," my mother said. "What do you know?" She turned to me. "Sweetheart, my parents—your Bubba and Zeyda—were born in Kiev. I was born in Salt Lake City. You were born in Overland Park."

My father finished her speech. "We're Jews. Wandering Jews. Our fate. Always and forever."

I stared at my bacon.

My mother bit off the crunchy end of one of her slices.

"You seem disappointed, Henry," she said. "Just because Donny is adopted doesn't mean you have to be too. I swear, I think the two of you spend too much time together." She swallowed. "You know what I think? Too much red hair in one place. It's downright dangerous." She and my father laughed again.

"Donny is adopted?"

"Of course he is," my mother said. "Didn't you know?"

"And I'm not?"

"Of course you're not."

My father raised his empty glass. "Pass me the OJ, son." I picked up the pitcher and remembered the condoms. If I'd had them in my pocket, I would have pulled them out and asked him, "What are these?" Donny told me they were dick shields. My mother told me they were balloons. What would Dad have to say? Everyone had a different version of everything.

At school the next morning, Donny was waiting for me at my locker. After I dialed the combination and opened the flimsy metal door, he raised his arm and rested his hand on top, giving me a full view of his armpit hairs. I was hoping that he did it on purpose.

"Hey."

"Hey."

"Tetherball after school?"

"Sure."

He lowered his arm and continued down the hall. I was exuberant. He made it so simple for us to not be finished.

"Are you or not?" he asked. He'd finished slamming the tetherball around the pole for another point, as if he needed one. He slammed and sweated and cursed, but he always won. I expected him to, and he did too.

"So?" His red hair was matted on his head. That's what happened to his hair on the second day that he didn't wash it, the longed-for second day when I'd try to come up with an excuse to move closer to him in order to smell him but didn't manage to do either, terrified that he might suspect something when he noticed my nostrils flaring to inhale more of him and I'd have to confess to him and myself why I would need to smell him and why I persisted in playing tetherball with him in the first place, since he always won. Neither of us was willing to reckon with that much. I was sure about that.

He unwound the rope, laid the ball to rest, and wiped the sweat off his forehead with the length of his lower arm. In the afternoon sunlight, the newly dampened hairs around his wrist glistened like the dewdrops of morning. I had to say something.

"No." It felt closed and safe. Donny struck the ball again, without his usual fervor. It made a weak revolution around the pole before bouncing against it a few times and coming to an undramatic standstill. I could have intercepted the ball easily and smacked it in my direction, but I didn't. We let it sit there, spent.

"I should be getting inside now," he said. "I would've won anyway."

"Okay."

He stepped outside the gravel court and onto the lawn. "You're such a loser." As he turned his torso in the direction of his house, I saw the sweat stain that had formed on the back of his shirt. It looked like a giant kidney, except that the bottom was pointy and made it look more like half a heart. I couldn't see his face, but as he walked away from me I heard him mutter something. It sounded like "faggot." I wasn't sure.

I froze in the small circle of our tetherball universe until it was clear that he wouldn't be looking back at me to unsay what he'd just said. I turned away too, toward my house. "Later!" I called out. He kept going without saying anything. Maybe he didn't hear me. Maybe he was done with me. I had to figure out how to be done with him, the bastard. If, while I watched him walk at a clip through his backyard toward the house, a UFO had beamed him up and taken him away, I might have pretended not to notice and continued on my way. But before he reached the azalea bushes where I fantasized about that happening, he darted to the left and disappeared on his own into the darkness. He was gone. Game over.

"Hen-ry!" I heard my mother's call. Dinner was ready. I cupped the tetherball between my hands. It was still warm and I could feel damp, oily blotches on it from our exertions. I tapped the ball counterclockwise and made it travel another weak revolution before it settled against the pole and I returned home for dinner.

SALISBURY STEAK WAS not one of my favorites, especially the globby sauce with canned button mushrooms that she smothered it in. What was she trying to hide? It was just a big hamburger to me, with stupid flavorless mushrooms on top. It did make me full.

"What were you and Donny up to?" It was the stock question my mother asked when I returned home after playing with Donny. No matter how many times she asked the question, it made me feel guilty about something I was supposed to confess and accept the consequences of.

"Tetherball."

"Who won?"

"He did."

Adrienne said, "Surprise surprise. Why do you even bother?"

"I'll win eventually."

"Don't hold your breath."

"I won't. You can hold your breath. Until you turn blue." I cut into the chunk of meat that had the most mushrooms on top. The mushrooms went down without triggering a gag reflex. I sliced off another piece of meat, much smaller this time, and scraped off all the mushrooms and sauce to see the surface of the meat. It was gray. I laid my fork and knife on my napkin. "Can I be excused? I'm not really hungry." I got up from the table and started walking away before Mom or Dad gave me permission to do so. I waited for someone to call me back or to follow me. No one said or did anything.

AFTER THE ADOPTION business, Donny and I stopped hanging out together in the neighborhood. The day would come. Our time together was a habit born out of convenience: he was my age; we needed to find things to do to pass the empty hours, which felt less empty in company; we believed that spending too much time alone was proof of not fitting in. We were able to relieve each other of these towering pressures. He had to know it, too. He wasn't an ace student, but he wasn't a fool. What he would never come to know was how the proximity of his physical presence, topped with his red hair, was enough for me to count the minutes until we were together again. I myself didn't come to know it until the school year was ending and he stopped me in the hallway to tell me that Becky had come over to his house.

"I didn't know you liked her."

"Are you kidding? Who doesn't like her? I never thought I stood a chance."

My schoolbooks were cradled against my chest like a bouquet of flowers. I lowered them to my side and secured their bottom edges with curled fingers, the boy way of holding books. "What did you do?"

"You mean what did I do to get her to come over? Or what did I do after she came over?"

What to say? He was leading me into a terrain of language and imagery that weren't mine. Or ours.

"Well?"

I didn't care how he got her to go to his house, but I was terrified of hearing what they did after she showed up. I wished I hadn't asked the question.

"She let me put one hand under her bra. I was so nervous I could barely feel what I was supposed to be feeling."

"What were you feeling?"

"I told you. Nervous." His fingers were fidgeting inside the pockets of his shorts and I was convinced he was struggling to push back an impulse of intimacy with me that was as strong as how I'd imagined it must feel if he were to abandon all restraint and clutch me tight, my face burrowed in the side of his neck, and hold me there long enough for me to be able to finally claim him as mine.

"You? Nervous?" I meant for the question to solicit trust. He pulled away and quickly found his way back to himself.

"Not to worry, man. I got over it. In a big way. A deep way, if you know what I mean." He bragged about how far he went with her, sparing no details, as if he needed to prove to me that he actually did the things he said he'd done. I didn't doubt that what he was telling me was true. In fact, I wanted him to continue. I wanted him to unravel his "deep way," which carried with it the possibility that he'd chosen me, and only me, to confide in, an intimacy that could prove deeper than his intimacy inside Becky.

"I got all the way. You know. To her cunt." He pronounced the word with bravado and then lost no opportunity to throw it about until he acquired a deftness in its use that suggested seasoned mastery. He didn't look me in the eye as he cunted along. His head turned slowly to the left and then to the right, as if his eyes were reaching toward a vaster audience made up of all the other guys he would tell at school the following day. I was only his dress rehearsal. That he had chosen me as his private audience signified a way of being intimate with me. But his way of intimacy wasn't my way. My way had him confessing that he didn't understand the big deal about the cunt, and then moving closer to me until his chest was against mine and he could wrap his arms around my back and push me against him until we melted into each other, and from there venture forth into the larger and scary world as one. Forever. But that wasn't his way.

"I'm gonna be late for Math," he said. "Anyway, I wanted

you to be the first to know." As he weaved through the other students making their way to class, I counted the number of times he slapped his hand against the buttocks of a teammate from football, basketball, baseball. After the seventh slap, he was lost in the shuffle of the other students. I surveyed the surface of heads for a sign of red hair popping up. Nothing. He was gone. I'd lost my idea of him, my hope for him, for us. If he should ever pass by me in the hall and go so far as to smack my ass, it would no longer carry the possibility of meaning that I hungered for it to mean. The secret desire that I didn't yet understand wasn't going to be made clear through him.

He retreated from me to safer zones of the classrooms we shared until school let out that year, stationing himself a few rows in front or in back of me, where it would require a deliberate act of intention for our eyes to meet. We stopped searching each other out after school. The rest of the year went by like that. I grew a little taller, my voice got deeper, and some hair finally grew on my legs and under my arms, slightly darker than the hair on my head but still within the spectrum of red. I was hoping for the burgeoning pubic hairs to grow thick and robust like those I imagined the men in the Sears catalog to be concealing beneath the underwear they were advertising and that I longed to pull down, like Donny said he did with Becky's. The two of them walked down the hall together arm in arm, ate in the cafeteria together, hovered together at their lockers. I caught them making out under the bleachers in the gym more than once. I saw his tongue slip into her mouth. Becky was a sweet girl. I hated her. From the moment she stole him from me, even if he wasn't mine to be stolen from, he was never near enough for me to be able to enjoy my secret pleasures of the particulars of him. Whenever I saw them together, my lungs collapsed and I couldn't breathe.

THAT SUMMER, THE Armstrongs moved to a state out west. I don't recall which one my mother mentioned, but her mouth opened wide when she enunciated the hard C at the beginning, followed by a string of syllables, and I thought, "Lucky him." Colorado? California?

"Transferred," she explained. "Bigger job. Better job. Higher salary. He deserves it. A good man. Good father. Good husband."

My father added, "All-around nice Irish guy." Mr. Armstrong scared me.

Donny's father died that summer too. After the move. Heart attack. The woman he was having an affair with called 911 after he'd released his hands from around her waist and brought them to his sternum, which he started pressing because of sharp pains that weren't letting up like they did whenever he had indigestion. When the ambulance arrived and the paramedics entered the motel room that the motel's reservation system showed he'd booked for every Tuesday night for the next two months (the night of the week that Donny's mother met with the other mothers of the book club she'd joined to try to make friends in the new neighborhood), he was already on the floor dead, clad in an unbuttoned Oxford cloth shirt and paisley boxers. The details buzzed about the neighborhood like the insects that were drawn to our illuminated patios and porches on summer nights. I was indifferent to the details, the hearsay. Everyone has a different version of everything. It was of no consequence to me whether he was fully dressed or buck naked when he dropped dead, or whether the blanket and top sheet were pulled back or still smooth on the mattress. The raw fact—Donny's father dropped dead in a motel room with another woman—was sufficient for me to know that Donny must be suffering and that my presence could be an elixir for his pain. I wanted him to suffer and to be denied the only remedy. Me. Serves him right. Let's see how he wins himself through this one. I was feeling defiant, victorious. Like Donny acted most of the time.

"Mr. Armstrong passed away," was all my mother had to

say about it at the dinner table as the four of us were passing around the platter of roast chicken and eyeing the choice pieces that we hoped hadn't been taken by the time the platter came our way. My mother and father were flexible. Adrienne and I fought over the drumsticks; the platter was moving clockwise, which meant that I had first dibs. An easy win.

"Yeah, I heard," I said, stabbing the larger of the two drumsticks with my fork and bringing it to my plate. I helped myself to a crispy wing as well.

My sister glared at me. "So, how'd you do on your English composition?"

"I got an A."

"That's my son," my mother said. "I knew you would." She asked if anyone wanted gravy. The three of us nodded our heads. She passed the gravy boat to me first, her prize child, the one she could count on to get an A on everything. A small lump of flour was floating on the surface. I spooned it up and deposited it on my napkin before pouring the gravy over my chicken. I banged my spoon against the napkin to make sure she noticed.

"Aren't we the fussbudget," she said. "Such a perfectionist."

"Actually, I didn't get an A on my composition. I got an F."

My father asked me to pass him the salt. As our hands met for the exchange, he asked, "Which is it? The A or the F?"

"The F. I didn't write a composition, so I got an F."

"I will not tolerate lying in this house!" he thundered. I paid him no mind. He dressed in Oxford cloth shirts every morning, sometimes with fancy cufflinks, before downing his breakfast half-standing up, grabbing his briefcase, and disappearing into a foreign world—industrial parks, offices, meetings. Motel rooms with women?

My mother took a sip of water. "What was the composition supposed to be on?"

"I don't know. I don't remember. Something about a book by Hemingway or Fitzgerald we were supposed to read that I didn't."

"Can you do extra credit to make it up?"

"I don't know."

My father turned to my mother. "Our son doesn't seem to know a helluva lot. Donny's influence. I told you you should have kept an eye on those two. They hung out together too much." Large beads of sweat had formed on his forehead. They were so repellent that my only desire was to distance myself from him until he was the size of a piece of dust. Donny had a sweaty forehead, too. It pulled me closer to him.

I pushed back my chair and rose from the table to leave. "You're right, Dad. I don't know much about anything."

"See?" my sister said. "He wants to be like Donny. He even wants to be adopted like Donny."

My eyes traveled a semicircle around the table, pausing at each member of my family to check for a sign of disturbance. All was calm. "Maybe I do." If one of them had broken the silence, I didn't hear them as I ran down the hall to my bedroom. I didn't want to know much of anything. I loved my mother and she loved me. I loved Donny and the idea of him loving me back one day. These two simple facts were all that I knew because they held my whole life. At the age of twelve or thirteen, they were enough. Knowing much of anything beyond that was too hard. There were too many versions of everything else.

BOOK TWO

One

From the window above our kitchen's double sink, I could see our son Toby sitting on top of the woodpile that my husband Len and I neatly stacked into a pyramid after Greg, our lawn guy, had taken a chainsaw to the row of Lombardy poplar trees and cut the felled monoliths into uniform blocks. The trees were old, their branches crusty and arched downward in frowns; a milky discharge dripped from the tips of their leaves.

"Stem canker, Henry," Greg said. "The leaf juice says it all."

"Is there a treatment?" Len asked.

"There is. It's pricey and there's no guarantee." What kind of guarantee was he referring to? Immortality?

Len pulled a leaf off one of the lower branches and rubbed it between his thumb and index finger. The milky liquid oozed out. He smelled his fingers. "Not nice," he said.

The trees were dying, but they weren't dead. "What do you think?" I asked them both.

"I think we should chop them down and dig out the root bulb," Len said. "Put an end to their suffering."

Greg nodded his head. "I can take care of it in the morning. I can't cart them away, unless you want me to rent a special truck and hire one of my men to help me. That's a lot of logs."

"We can keep the logs. Stack them in the side yard," I said. "We can use them in the fireplace."

"Who knows if the fireplace still works. Did your folks ever use it?" Len asked me.

"Not while I was growing up."

"We'll need to see if it's still functional," he said. "Things forget how to work if they're not used."

"If the logs end up sitting there, Toby'll find a way to have fun on them. For him, it'll be a giant Lego."

The fireplace didn't work, and Toby loved climbing the woodpile when he was younger. Each foothold was an adventure with its own treacheries as he made his ascent to the summit. Len called the pile "Mount Lombardy" and insisted that one of us keep an eye on Toby as he played on the wood. Toby had his share of scrapes and falls. He didn't make a fuss about his miscalculations. He'd run to us, repeating "Booboo." A dampened tissue gently blotting the blood, a peck on the cheek, and he was ready to get back to business.

Toby got bored with Mt. Lombardy after a year or so, about the same time that Len and I forgot about the fireplace in the living room. Toby returned to the woodpile when he was twelve. He no longer had to climb it. He leapt onto the top, twisting his lithe body in mid-air and landing on his bum. I liked to watch him sitting there from the kitchen window, especially when he was by himself. When he was with a friend, there was a lot of chatter going on and I wasn't much interested in what they were saying. Goofy stuff, most likely. He was only twelve. But when he was alone, he was tucked into himself, working through something private, I thought as I tried to return to the dishes in the sink and failed. I couldn't resist watching him, as if it were my duty to nab those glimpses of early drafts of him. After all, I was his father and he was at a difficult age. The Age of Donny—or Toby's version of it, whatever it might be.

"Are you probing and dissecting again?" Len asked me

whenever he caught me observing our son as if he were a microbe in a petri dish. On this occasion in the kitchen, he snuck up on me from behind, the spy spying on the spy.

"Just keeping an eye."

"Leave him alone. He's fine."

"How do you know?"

"I don't," he said. "How do you know he might not be?"

"I don't. That's why I keep an eye on him."

He rested his hands on my shoulders and swiveled me until I was facing him. "Henry," he said, "how about looking at your husband instead? I happen to be fine. Take advantage of it." He moved his lips toward mine. "Give the kid some breathing space so I can take yours away." We kissed above the dirty dishes. I kept my eyes open to see if he was doing the same. He was. He was intent on me. I was intent on him too, except for an instant when I shifted my eyes to the right so that I could peer out the window to see whether Toby could see us. I wasn't sure whether I wanted him to or not. Len didn't notice my deviation, or he pretended not to notice. I finished rinsing the dishes in the morning.

When Toby was on the woodpile with B.J., the two of them sat closer together than Toby did with his other friends. Once, I saw Toby tousle B.J.'s head of unruly hair. B.J. smiled and didn't take the trouble to pull away. They must do this kind of thing a lot. To be privy to what they were talking about would have been delicious, but they were too far away to hear anything. When they were together, my radar was on high alert.

The "B" stood for Brian. His parents had told me, and I called him by his full name whenever he stopped by.

"What does the 'J' stand for?" I asked Toby one night over dinner. "His last name is Snyder, isn't it?"

"Snyderman. The J is probably for his middle name. No way he'd be called 'B.S.'"

"What's his middle name?"

"Beats me. Jay, John, Jack." He paused. "Jerk-off for all I

know. What difference does it make?"

"More salad?"

"Why would I want more salad?" He was in a mood.

Len came to the rescue. "For nourishment without bulk. We're jogging tomorrow after school. This time through the Wissahickon, down the bridle path and all the way to the Schuylkill River." He added, "You can bring B.J. if you want."

"He's got football practice tomorrow. Big game on Saturday."

"Are you going?" I asked.

"Why would I do that?" He shoved too much romaine into his mouth. The frilly ends fell back into his plate and a rivulet of ranch dressing worked its way down his chin. It didn't occur to him to pick up his napkin and wipe it off. "I hate football. So boring."

I looked at Len for the guidance that I'd come to expect from his eyes whenever they focused on me too long. He met my glance and got up to clear the table. "I'm not a football fan either," he said. I rose to help him.

"Thank you," I whispered to him at the sink.

"Don't get so worked up," he said. "He's trying to hate us."

"Why would he want to do that?"

"Because he's twelve. It'll pass. Don't tell me you can't remember what it was like." He found my hand under the suds in the sink and weaved his fingers between mine. "You of all people. You and your Danny."

"Donny."

"Donny."

Len had a point.

Toby wasn't keen on football. He preferred swimming and wrestling and made junior varsity for both. I couldn't understand how the two sports fit together. Swimming was a solitary business, physical exertion dissolving in the balm of the water and the soft choreography of breath and stroke. Wrestling was the hard impact of two bodies and the merging and assault of flesh and sweat. In Toby, the two incompatibilities cohabited as if there were nothing more natural in the world. When he came out of a race or a match, I focused on his blue eyes, which made me imagine vast Caribbean seas and the mysterious ecosystems they nourished deep within. He had Len's eyes, so much so that he could have glided through life without ever having to pause to consider whether he was adopted. Except for the fact that he had two dads.

"A WARNING," AMANDA told us. "The birth certificate will have 'Baby Boy' or 'Baby Girl' on it. We can change it once you decide on a name." We liked our social worker's name. Amanda. We added it to the "girl" column of our name list.

Len and I started the list a few weeks before the birth. After dinner, we'd sit on the living room sofa and stare into space until a name emerged that made both of us nod our heads. Len would write it on the pad of yellow legal-size paper we kept on the side table next to the sofa. "I'll be the scribe," he said. "Your handwriting is illegible." We considered consulting a book of baby names. Len told me the approach was inorganic. "The name will come to us," he said.

Toby stuck. Our friend Megan proposed it one evening as I was opening a second bottle of red wine. We agreed that it was a simple name, short and classy, different but not strange, and it would work for a girl or a boy. Len and I decided not to be told the sex of our child until it was born.

"Are you sure you don't want to know?" Amanda asked us. "It could make things easier. You know, the baby clothes, the color of the nursery, the teenager phase. You know." We did like her name, although we worried that people might call our child Mandy. Three-syllable names have a tendency to shrink to an inelegant one- or two-syllable alternative. We shared the same concerns about two of our favorites: Zachary and Eleanor.

"Look what happened to me," Len said.

"I can call you Le-o-nard if you want."

"Too late for that, Henry," he said. "Unless I can call you Hen."

Len was the one who'd introduced the idea of adopting. I wasn't against it, but I wasn't jumping at it either. I'd never thought about it before. "Two men and a baby?" I asked him when he told me he wanted us to raise a child together.

He brought up the subject regularly, though usually out of nowhere, and would then look at me and say, "So?" He'd drag the word out as if it was far greater than the sum of its two letters. We'd talk about it. He called me a pessimist. I claimed to be realistic. I called him a dreamer. He claimed to be realistic. He said it was very serious, which was why a bit of lightness was in order. "Lighten up," he'd tell me.

He persisted in this gentle, easy way for a few months until I came around.

"Sure," I finally said. "Why not?"

He did the same thing to get me to move in with him. It was his way. So simple. I loved it. I loved him, especially the ease of him. I only hoped the baby would be easy too, even if I had no idea what that meant.

We moved to a larger apartment before the birth of Baby Boy. Our one-bedroom apartment was the standard urban fare of young singles or couples who believed themselves to be light-years away from having to consider the practicalities of housing children: large bedroom, galley kitchen, spacious living room for entertaining, one bathroom with shower/sauna combination. During the time we lived there, our circle of married friends gradually narrowed, couple by couple, as they abandoned Center City for the suburbs once parenthood had been confirmed. They spoke of yards and swing sets year-round, of inflatable pools in summer, ice-skating rinks in winter, and good school districts. What they explained didn't need to be explained. It made sense. Nevertheless, we were intent on remaining in the buzz of a city while we relished the tiny pulse of an infant's heartbeat against our chests. Len was in real estate and had established himself in high-end condos. I organized local events, whose ebbs and flows averaged out to a decent income. As a financial collective, we felt secure enough to make an offer on a pricey two-bedroom, two-bathroom condo facing a well-maintained square appointed with benches and a small playground with a pea gravel surface under all of the apparatus—sliding board, jungle gym, Jacob's ladder, balance beams. Seasonal flowering shrubs lined the patches of green and the pedestrian walkways. We negotiated a decent price because the unit was on the third floor of the twenty-story building. Although the rooms were bright, the sky wasn't visible at eye level from the window. Also, Len had connections for this particular unit. Some of his connections were shady, I suspected, because he referred to them as "This guy I know." If we found ourselves struggling to make ends meet, we could always bleed into the exodus of our friends.

"Let's do it," he said. "Why not?"

"Why not?"

We made the move. The baby was born. We told Amanda that we'd chosen a name for Baby Boy.

"Toby," we said in unison.

"Toby it will be," she replied. "I'll take care of the paperwork. Now get some rest, especially Len. You've lost some weight, haven't you?"

Len, my improbable partner. Tall and skinny, the shapeless gawky kind; more cute than handsome, sweet, drama-free. Easy. Everything I wasn't looking for when I met him. Except his very blue eyes. We met at a party of a mutual acquaintance—was it Adam?—whom I dated and slept with twice before it became evident that nothing more could come of us except a friendly happenstance intersection, such as this one, an invitation to his promotion celebration. Adam had finally succeeded in having the word "Associate" removed from his job title at the law firm where he worked.

I was standing by the hors d'oeuvre table reaching for a

deviled egg to give me a sense of purpose while I surveyed the room, looking for someone I might know.

"Here. You might need this," a man said, extending a cocktail napkin. There was nothing flirtatious in his voice, but he was smiling and his eyes were too.

He handed me the napkin, turned, and walked to the empty balcony, where he rested his elbows on the ledge and gazed at the night sky as if that was all the company he needed. For such a skinny guy, he had a round bum. I stood at the table eating my deviled egg and feeling conspicuous in my solitude. He seemed comfortable in his, and I wondered how he managed it. I made my way to the balcony.

"Thanks for the napkin. It came in handy." I opened the napkin to show him the flecks of paprika and dots of mayonnaise that would have finished on my face if he hadn't anticipated my needs.

"You're welcome." His eyes were cast downward. I imagined him struggling to be flirtatious, as if he were trying it out for the first time. He did smile again, though, and I noticed a crooked upper front tooth. I found it appealing, but then wondered whether, unlike his searing blue eyes, it was the kind of quirky attraction that inevitably would turn against me and become another irritation. I don't remember what we talked about on the balcony, even though we remained there as the other guests were thinning out. I left the party before he did, and as I turned away from him I decided, "No way am I going to fall in love with this guy." I turned around to look at him again. He was resting on the edge of the balcony again. "But I could slip into love with him. That sounds healthier." I went back to the balcony and gave him my number.

He called a week later. We went on a few dates before we had sex. We moved in together after a year. "I can move into your place," he said. "It's big enough, and I don't have much. It'll be easy." I had nothing against the idea of ease. It was new to me and sounded promising, but I wasn't a firm believer.

"Let's find a new place," I said. "I don't want you fitting yourself around my stuff."

"Sure. That makes sense." We chose an apartment that was smaller than mine.

Two years later, we were married. Three years after that, we adopted. Our "pregnancy" was about reams of paperwork and interrogation that suggested we were guilty of some heinous infraction. Len was up to the task. "Take it easy," his eyes told me each time a form was laid before us to be read and signed, each time a social worker came for a home visit. "We're guilty of nothing." Papers were signed, home visits passed without incident. Nothing unsettling happened in the process except one thing: my growing belief in ease, entirely attributable to Len, my improbable husband, my antidote to much of me.

LEN AND I were in agreement about not depositing our son in preschool for as long as our careers permitted. Too many germs, too little individual care. We opted for the full throttle of parental immersion, taxing as it might be.

"You know how my schedule can be," he said. "The burden will fall mostly on you."

"So will the pleasure."

When Toby was able to toddle, I let him loose at the playground in the park across the street while I staked out an unoccupied bench to read a book that wouldn't be engrossing enough to make me forget I had a son to keep an eye on. He had his share of tumbles and scrapes in the playground as he did on the woodpile. "Mommy!" he'd call out until he reached the harbor of me, set anchor at my feet and docked his head between my legs. His miniature frame molded itself against me, and I'd stroke his wavy hair, saying nothing until his quivering subsided and he withdrew his head from my legs to look way up to my face. He was waiting for me to bend down, kiss both cheeks, shift my lips to one of his ears, and whisper the two magic words, as I always did.

"All better."

Off he'd go to rejoin the other kids. I'd open my book and resume my reading, lifting an eye after each paragraph to check on him and to scan the groupings of women on the benches. Surely some of them weren't the mothers of the children they were watching over. Not in this neighborhood with its high-end park. I listened for foreign accents. Nannies who'd been "brought in" were in vogue.

One afternoon, I watched as Toby stumbled on the gravel path between the jungle gym and the sliding board. He caught himself before his knees grazed the small white stones, but he still came running toward me. In front of him were two other children running toward the women who'd brought them to the park. He tried to catch up with them, calling "Mommy" as they were doing, but they were too far ahead. Their cries subsided as soon as they slammed into two women who hadn't risen from the benches but had simply bent over and extended their arms as if they were holding a skein. Toby slammed into me and burrowed himself into my lower half. I said, "All better." He continued to mutter "Mommy." Something else was going on.

"Where's my mommy?"

I gazed into his blue eyes, their sclera etched with fine red veins that resembled a map delineating all the countries of a large continent whose many languages and dialects were gibberish to me. In my peripheral vision, I could see a child approaching. He tapped Toby on the shoulder.

"Wanna play?" In his other hand, he held a small truck, one that probably came inside a cereal box.

Toby took the truck. "Where's your mommy?"

The boy pointed to a bench where three women were seated. "There's my mommy," he said. "The pretty one."

They ran off together and I looked at the three women in the distance. They were all pretty.

Len was home on the afternoon when Toby asked again. It must have been a Saturday or Sunday. He'd been in kindergarten for a few months. He and I were sitting at the kitchen table waiting for Len to finish spreading mayonnaise on the turkey sandwiches he was fixing for lunch at the counter. Len had a habit of spreading the mayonnaise on the surface of the meat and not on the bread. He did the same with mustard and ketchup. I meant to ask him why he did it that way, but each time I was about to ask him, I realized the answer held no import.

"Apple juice?" I asked Toby as I reached for his glass.

"No thanks," he said, glancing toward Len. "Dad, where's my mommy?"

Len arrived at the table with the sandwiches. "I don't know, son," he said. "Where's your napkin?"

"Right here on the table."

"Please put it on your lap. Or tuck it under your chin."

Toby looked toward me.

"I don't know either. Lap is fine."

He placed the napkin on his lap without unfolding it and grabbed the dish of potato salad. "What's that green stuff in it?"

"Parsley," Len said. We waited for Toby to reject the dish. He wasn't fond of green food, except for sour pickles and string beans.

Toby separated a piece of the parsley from the potato salad with his fingers and let it linger on his tongue. "Weird," he said.

"Kind of," Len said. "Weird bad or weird good?"

He extracted another piece of parsley and chewed on it. "It's okay. Pretty good." And another. "I think I like it."

We sat there eating our sandwiches and potato salad. Without asking him again, I filled Toby's glass with apple juice. He drank it down straight away. I poured him a second glass and started returning the pitcher to the coaster.

"I'll have some too," Len said. When his hand met mine halfway, he made a point of wrapping his long slender fingers around mine and giving them a gentle squeeze. It was his way of saying, "Look at me, please." And I did, expecting his eyes to be already gazing at mine, their icy blue radiating heat and waiting to connect with mine and make me love him all over again as if for the first time. Len's eyes. Toby's eyes. A sheer coincidence of intense blue that created an affinity between them which was off-limits to me, what with my mother's brown cow eyes. I didn't mind being relegated to secondary parent. It eased the burden.

That night, in bed, Len said to me, "He finally asked us. Here we go."

"What do we do?"

"Nothing. He was the one to change the subject. Long live parsley. He'll let us know if he needs more."

"What'll we tell him when he needs more?"

"Beats me. Maybe he won't need more." He laid on top of me and pressed his groin into mine. "Can you believe it," he said, "he actually ate parsley." After he worked his tongue inside my mouth to prevent me from saying anything, he shifted himself so that we were in a sixty-nine position. "Let's try something new," he said.

"We've done this before."

"I have a variation for tonight."

TOBY PUSHED INTO adolescence, which was undeniable when I detected hair under his armpits at the same time that I noticed wisps of gray hair at my temples. He spent as much time as possible away from Len and me, although Len assured me over and over that he needed us even more. "Only in the background, though," he advised. "That's where our place is going to be for a while. Better get used to it."

He was right. I was proficient at keeping in the shadows

of our teenage son. But on this particular night in the kitchen, as I watched our son on the woodpile staring into the sky, Len was out with a client. I was free to go about my business unchecked. How easy it would be to slip outside for a bit of fresh air. How natural it would be to follow the flagstone path that led from the back door to the property line on the right, where the woodpile was. How surprised I could pretend to be when I happened onto Toby on the woodpile. I let the dish I was washing glide back under the sudsy layer of sink water and went out the back door, making sure to be peering up at the universe before happening upon the universe of our teenage son.

The half-moon was unobstructed by clouds. The light it emanated with the help of the stars etched its shadowed half. "Nice night," I said.

"Yep."

"Great stars," I said.

"Yep."

"Do you want to be alone?" I asked.

"Not if I had my choice. You?"

"I could go either way," I said.

He turned toward the street as if he were looking for something, expecting something, expecting someone. B.J.? "You can stay here if you want."

"If you want me to."

In the darkness, I could imagine the blue of his eyes. "Jesus, Pop," he said. "Stay here or don't. Why do you have to make everything so complicated?"

I rested my hand on his knee. "I didn't want to intrude. That's all."

"I said I didn't want to be alone, didn't I?"

"Maybe it wasn't my company you wanted."

"There you go again," he said as he shifted to the left. My hand slipped off his knee.

"Sorry, son." I put my hand back on his knee.

"It's okay, Pop." He put his hand on top of mine. "Grandma had this thing about knees too. And cheeks. She couldn't resist squeezing them. Her hands were rougher than yours."

"You remember that?"

"Yep."

"Do you miss her?"

"Kind of."

"I do too."

"Duh. She was your mother."

"What else do you remember about her?"

He lifted the leg that my hand was resting on so that it formed a triangle. My hand slid down his knee to his calf. I could feel some leg hair there. "Not much. Her breath smelled like lemons."

"She liked to suck on her lemon candies."

"She called me 'Tobileh.' That's Yiddish, right? And oh, her hair was light blue. Was that natural?"

"When her hair started turning gray, she had it colored."

"But blue?"

"That's what they did then."

"Not blue the way she had it done. Her hair was blue blue."

"Like your eyes."

He lowered his leg. My hand dropped back to my side.

"My blue is natural."

I was about to tell him how much she loved him when two bright lights blinded us from the darkness of the night. Len pulling into the driveway.

"Let's greet him," I said.

"You go. I'll stay here for a while. It's fun to watch you guys get corny when you see each other." As I walked down the driveway to meet Len, Toby called out, "Grandma was corny too."

I opened the front door of the car and bent down to give Len a peck on the cheek. "What did I miss?" he asked.

"Not much," I said. "But I could be wrong."

Toby waved at us.

"Go over and ask our son," I said to Len as he loosened his grip on me. "He probably has a different take on things. I need to go back in and rinse the dishes."

Len climbed onto the woodpile and fit himself against Toby as snug as tongue-and-groove. I let my hands feel their way among the dishes and utensils soaking in the warm sink water while my eyes focused on the two men in my life out there in the dark. I could make out lips moving incessantly in the silence, fingers and legs fidgeting in the stillness. Could they be arguing? When I finished the last of the dishes, they were still perched on the woodpile. Toby's head was resting against Len's shoulder. I dimmed the kitchen light and stood watching them framed in an immense darkness pierced by the pinpricks of stars. A perfectly rendered still-life of a good life. Our life.

Two

As soon as my mother settled into the suburbs, she lost all desire to venture into densities of humanity. Her city legs and spirit retracted into her body. The mere suggestion of going into town made her twitch like some sea creature washed ashore and flailing for oxygen. "If you want to see me again, it'll have to be at my house," she said on her second visit to Len's and my apartment.

"Except when you come to our wedding," I said. "Right off of Broad and Walnut."

"Is it easy to park there?"

"There'll be valet parking and the reception is only two blocks away."

She shrugged her shoulders.

"She says your apartment is cramped and that outside is a bunch of noise and dirt," my father told me as they were leaving our place after dinner that night. "Can't argue that."

"I could."

"I know, I know. She can't get past it." He passed a hand through his thinning, graying hair and made me wonder if that was what was in store for me. "I'll keep working on her. Your mother. She's a project all right, but don't worry. She'll be at your wedding."

She did come to the wedding. Every time I surveyed the

reception hall to see where she was and whether she was brooding, she was in company and appearing to have a grand old time.

My father died six months after Len and I were married. He was sixty and played tennis three mornings a week, out-fitted from head to toe in Sergio Tacchini athletic wear. His upper thighs and arms exhibited more sinew than Len's and mine taken together; not a trace of belly or spare tire. He was enjoying his early retirement. His eyes sparkled through the cataracts that he wouldn't get removed.

"I can see everything I need to," he said whenever I brought up the subject of surgery. I let it go.

I was more adamant about him having a PSA. "I pee when I have to. I stand at the toilet and guess what happens. Pee comes out. What's the problem?"

I spoke to my mother about the PSA test. I made a point of repeating the acronym. She took acronyms seriously. I could count on her to shift into nagging mode with my father. It was her privilege and her right. She was his wife of almost half a century.

It must have been winter when she called me and the swift unraveling of my father kicked in: The afghan my grand-mother had knitted was spread across my lap while I was reading a book after dinner, and it was already dark outside. "Your father's primary care doctor called me after his phys-ical today," she said. "Dr. Patel. I think you've met him. The Indian one."

I closed the book without folding the corner to mark my place and tucked the afghan under my thighs. "What did he say?"

"He still refuses to have a PSI," she said. "Men his age are supposed to have one. Can you talk to him again? You're a man."

"It's PSA, Mom. Sure. I'll work on it."

"I pee fine," my father said. "And I don't wake up because I have to pee. Bad dreams wake me up. Your mother's snoring wakes me up. And when I wake up, I say to myself, 'May as well pee while I'm up.' Makes sense, no?"

I didn't respond right away.

"Len doesn't snore?"

"Dad, a PSA is no big deal. You sit in a chair for a minute while they draw blood. End of story. You don't even have to fast."

"Will you stop badgering me if I do it?"

"Promise."

The result came back three days after he had his blood drawn: 7. Way out of range to be brushed off. Dr. Patel referred him to a urologist, who conducted a rectal examination. "A couple of rough patches on the prostate," he said. "I don't want to sound alarmist, but I think you should have a biopsy." My father agreed once he verified that his health plan network covered the cost.

I accompanied him to the follow-up appointment. "You're clean," the urologist said. "Good to go." He shook my father's hand. "When you take care of your copay at the check-out desk, schedule another PSA in about six months."

My father would have been good to go if it hadn't been for the bacteria residing on the spring-driven needle biopsy device. When the needle was injected, the microorganisms detected fertile ground in my father's bloodstream, where they sent out tiny shoots of a staph infection that coursed through his veins, blossomed into septicemia, and killed him. My mother and I discussed a lawsuit. Len reminded us that we had enough money. He also convinced us to tell everyone my father died of a stroke if they asked. "Everyone will give their condolences and leave it at that," he said. "Isn't that what you would want?" He had a point.

On the last day of sitting shiva, Len and I invited my mother to stay with us. Len and I were seated on our black leather sofa, my mother on its charcoal twin facing us.

"Where will I sleep? In the bathtub? You trying to kill me too?"

Len draped one arm over my shoulders, let his hand settle onto my deltoid and squeezed it hard enough to give me pain. It was his way of stopping me in my tracks, of warning me that I was entering into a no-exit zone. I looked at him as if to say, "What the fuck!" He looked back as if to say, "Shut up." Then he abandoned me, sidled up to my mother and wrapped his arms around her. "We want you to be with us until you're back on your feet."

She squeezed his cheeks and kissed his forehead. "Nice try, *shayna punim*. I'm not budging."

LEN LOOKED FORWARD to going to the house I grew up in, from the day he made his first cursory tour of the house and spent an hour in my bedroom examining every object on display. He called the house "The Museum of the Henry." He should have been an anthropologist. The laundry room was his favorite. There, he bent over the washing machine to get a closer look at the family snapshots on the wall. Some were thumbtacked; others were taped along their top edge; the special ones were framed and hung on hooks.

"The Ancient History collection," I replied. "Pretty standard stuff." The largest photo was my high school graduation picture. It hung above the dryer along with my sister's. "Everyone parted their hair in the middle back then." I leaned closer. "And they made all of my pimples disappear."

"You had pimples?"

"You didn't?" I ran my finger along the satin-finish glass. Not a trace of dust on my fingertip. Leave it to my mother.

"I didn't have pimples and I didn't wear a part."

"You couldn't. You had frizzy hair."

"And I still do." He bent closer to scrutinize a snapshot of Donny and me in the above-ground pool. Donny was sitting on my shoulders trying to push my head under the water. "His hair was frizzy, too. You have a thing for frizz, don't you?"

"My downfall."

"Downfall? Have you fallen down?"

"Don't think so." I ran my fingers through Len's hair. Did Donny's have the same unkempt thickness? I smelled the tips of my fingers to see if that would help me remember.

My mother came into the laundry room and caught us in my act of tenderness. She extended her index finger toward a photo of me racing down the hill in the back yard in my go-cart. I couldn't have been more than ten. "Wasn't he adorable?"

"He sure was," Len said. "Still is. Most of the time."

"This is one of my favorites," she said, removing one of the smaller framed photos from the wall. "Look at the two of them jammed into the tree with a box of Ritz crackers. They didn't need anything else in the world, the little devils."

"They probably didn't," Len said. "Donny and Henry." He ran the three words together as if they were one.

"Donny's probably bald by now," I said.

Len ran his fingers through my hair. "Yours is getting there."

My mother turned away from us. "Come to the kitchen. There's apple strudel waiting." As she scurried off, Len told me that he was hoping for poppy seed cake and then introduced the subject of having a baby for the first time.

"Hurry up, boys," she called. "I took it out of the oven."

I stood at the washing machine waiting for Len to continue.

"It's what couples do and what widowed mothers-in-law need," was all he had to say before he grabbed my hand and pulled me toward the aroma of cinnamon coming from the kitchen. "On our way, Mom!" he hollered.

TOBY WAS FIVE days old when we brought him home. The day after, my mother came to visit. She took the train into town. Len agreed to meet her at the station and I agreed to drive her home after a dinner of brisket with kasha and bow-ties for the adults, Enfamil for the baby. When I heard the front door unlocking, I rushed down the hallway with Toby cradled in one arm. She extended her arms. "Give him to me," she said, "and take this for me." Behind her were two matching pieces of cherry-red Samsonite luggage.

She stayed for two weeks. Twice a day, the three of us ventured to the park across the street, where there were scads of babies, all of them with women. The few men in the park were on their own and fell into two types—the suit-and-tie ones negotiating a take-out cup of coffee in one hand and a cellphone in the other; or the homeless ones settled under a tree with a large backpack or shopping cart parked against the trunk. I found some of the men from each type sexy, others less so, and others not at all. It was the homeless men who held my attention as I tried to make up a story about how they got to be where they were. If my mother and son weren't with me, I might have approached one of them, one of the younger ones, the sexier ones, with the excuse of finding out.

We stationed ourselves on any bench that was unoccupied and played a game that we called "Who's a mother and who's a nanny?" The game made my mother smile a lot. Sometimes she even burst into laughter, which had the effect of unleashing her younger self and mine. Lovely moments, those. On her final night with us, we arranged for our as yet untried babysitter, Chloe, to stay with Toby so that we could take Mom out to dinner. Chloe lived in the building. Her parents were rich. She'd confessed to us one night that she wanted to make money for things she absolutely had to have that her parents didn't approve of and wouldn't pay for.

"Nonsense," my mother said. "You two go. I can take care of the baby. God knows you need a night out to yourselves." I told her the restaurant was around the corner and authentic Italian.

"Do they have cannellonis?"

"The best. And it's 'cannelloni,' Mom."

She agreed. After dinner, she insisted on paying the bill. When we arrived home, she insisted on paying Chloe. We let her.

When Chloe closed the front door behind her, the three of us entered our bedroom, where Toby was sleeping in his crib. "Look at him," Mom said. I could sense it coming, the lament that continually snagged her like a rough fingernail against a nylon stocking: "If only your father were here."

"I'll go and get the car," I told her. "Len, why don't you grab the suitcases."

She made the train ride once a week, and within a few months she was spending half of her time with us in the city, taking the Amtrak local on Tuesday afternoons and leaving on Friday afternoons. We no longer needed Chloe; the few times I ran into her in the elevator or lobby, I greeted her politely. She didn't seem to mind. She must have found other gigs to make money. Everything on her looked just-bought.

When Toby was three and we ventured with the stroller on the 24th Street bridge, over the Schuylkill River and into West Philadelphia, my mother stopped and extended her hand the way a crossing guard does. Her eyes were focused on the façade of 30th Street Station. "What a stunning building," she said. "Your father would love this." She looked down at the stroller. "He should be here."

When Toby was five, she was supposed to come with us to pick him up from his first day at kindergarten, even though it was a Monday. "I can pick her up at the station," Len said. "It's my turn."

A few days before, I'd driven to the suburbs to take her to Dr. Patel. She'd been complaining about heartburn. "The Maalox doesn't do shit," she said.

The doctor explained that she had arrhythmias. "Erratic and disorganized impulses are being fired from her ventricles." I had no idea what he was saying, but he arranged for her to go directly from his office to the hospital. I stayed with her until Len arrived in the late afternoon.

On my last visit before she died, she motioned me to the bed. "I gave you a hard time," she said, reaching for my hand and squeezing it. The pressure felt more like anger than love. "I always thought it would be you and Donny. That tiny secret love of yours worried me so. But it grew into Len. And you and Len have a son. Your little secret burst forth and the world doesn't give a hoot." She struggled for another deep breath. "If your father had been around longer, everything would have been easier for me. For you. Forgive me."

I extracted my hand and let it travel up her arm, following a pronounced blue vein that disappeared under the tunnel of the sleeve of her hospital gown as it made its way to her heart. Her lunch was laid out on the bed tray across her belly—boneless chicken breast, green beans, mashed potatoes, rice pudding, and a thimble-sized pill cup holding two blue capsules.

"I'm not hungry," she said as I started to peel the plastic wrapping off the meal tray.

"You should eat."

"Christ, you sound like me," she said, pushing my hand away from her meal. "Do yourself a favor. Make it a point not to sound so much like me."

I returned my hand to the spot on her upper arm where the big blue vein burrowed under the tunnel of her sleeve. I imagined the oxygen-deprived blood coursing through that vein, fighting the erratic and disorganized impulses that Dr. Patel had described as it made its way to her heart. Her very broken heart.

"IF YOU MANAGE the estate, you can have everything," Adrienne told me. "All I want is Mom's engagement ring and the mezuzah on the front door. You can do what you want with the rest. Keep it, sell it, give it away, throw it away." She had a busy life far away in Battle Creek, Michigan. I'd never gone to visit her because of the frenetic pace of her life that she dramatized during our weekly phone calls. If she was so busy and important, what would I do with myself in Battle Creek? Take a guided tour of the Kellogg's corn flakes plant? Besides, my sister didn't interest me all that much. Neither did her second husband, Kevin. He was a regional sales representative for a product line having to do with processed chicken or cheese and made decent money like Adrienne. They didn't have children. I didn't ask her why. I'd never asked her why about anything having to do with her. She wasn't the type to be challenged about herself. From the time we were teenagers, her nails were always polished, her lips always glossy. She was a creature of surfaces. I dabbled in rough edges. We grew apart during our teenager phase. We continued to make each other laugh, sometimes uncontrollably, and didn't ever fight. But we weren't close. Mom died during what Adrienne claimed was her busiest period. "I have four closings next week!" she said breathlessly. I understood that she wanted nothing to do with the logistics of a death. Who does? Still.

"If you decide to sell the house, I'll take the listing," she said.

"You're in Michigan. How would you show it?"

"Not to worry. I have my people."

"Okay, sis."

We didn't give her the listing. No one got the listing.

"Let's move in," Len said, squeezing by me in our galley kitchen to put an empty glass in the sink. I didn't feel his groin being playful against my bum as he slid through. He must be serious.

"Are you out of your mind?"

He turned on the hot water spigot as he let loose with phrases like "more space," "fresh air," "good schools," phrases I'd heard often and which used to make us roll our eyes in collusion. This time, however, he was on the other side.

"Our friends may have had a point. Your mother, too.

The apartment is too small. I think we've outgrown it. We're breathing down each other's necks."

"And avoiding each other's groin areas."

"Think about it," he said. "Split-level. It sounds roomy."

Toby ran into the kitchen. "Are we moving to the big house?" He heard everything. "When? Can I have a swing set with a sliding board?"

"Good thinking," Len said. "For you and the new friends you'll make."

"How many friends will I make?"

"How about starting with one?" Len looked at me. "Sometimes you don't need more than that if it's the right one."

"How will I know?"

"You'll just know," he said. "Like with Pop and me."

Toby looked at us. "But you're not friends."

"We're not?"

"You're married. That's different."

"Okay then. How about like with Dad and his buddy Donny?"

"Who's Donny?"

"Ask Dad."

"So are we?" Toby looked at Len as he made his way toward me. I reached down to scoop up our son. He wrapped his arms around my shoulders, his legs around my waist. The tightness, the constriction. More space, private space. It made sense.

WE DISPOSED OF my parents' furniture and appurtenances. Len and I had enough of our own history to distribute among the rooms. The L-shaped sofa was the one point of contention. I wanted to keep it.

"Why?" Len asked me. "How often did you sit on it?" He sat down on the side that didn't lean against the wall. "It isn't even comfortable. What am I supposed to do with my head?"

"You could always stick it up your ass." I sidled up to him.

"The fabric is hideous."

"We can have it reupholstered."

He kissed me on the forehead. "Fess up. What did you and Donny do on this sofa?"

"Nothing."

"What were you hoping to do with him on the sofa?"

"You know the answer to that. Everything."

Donny at school. Donny in the yard. Donny in the pool. Donny never on the sofa but almost behind the sofa. Len knew a thing or two about first love. He knew he couldn't compete with my Donny. He'd had his Donny too. Everyone had their Donny, the person you hoped to discover everything about love through. He knew he wasn't that for me, just as he knew that I wasn't that for him. We'd arrived at each other too late for that, but along the way we'd learned a thing or two about love, the drunkenness of it, the sobriety of it, the frequent transactional demands it imposes to keep it strong and healthy.

"We can keep the sofa," Len said, "if I can choose new fabric."

"What if I hate it?"

"You won't."

"So you agree. The sofa stays."

I didn't hate the slate-gray color or the combination linen/microfiber sample he brought home; I didn't love it either.

"It's fine," I said.

"We can go a shade darker if you want. Add a smidgeon of walnut. To match your eyes."

"Perfect," I replied. "I always wanted my eyes to resemble a sofa. Let's stick with the sample. It won't show dirt and it'll last. We might actually use the sofa."

"When we invite all the new friends we make."

"Jerk." I ran my left hand across the rust- and gold-striped upholstery of one of the cushions. It was thick and scratchy, with little lumps of matted fabric dotted throughout. Clearly uncomfortable. But familiar. Who knew whether Donny had moved back to the area?

Three

My thirty-year high school reunion was held at the Copper Kettle Inn, a restaurant that specialized in steak soup served in individual ceramic bowls with a single thumb-shaped handle on one side. At least it did some forty years ago when my parents took Adrienne and me there. It must have been a special occasion for them to venture beyond the neat ring of suburbs into Blue Bell, a zone that had spread slowly and organically over two centuries before the advent of the suburbs. Large stone houses barely visible among the density of towering trees that had taken root even centuries before the settlers had claimed several acres of land as their own. A zone cloaked in a stretch of history that the hastily manufactured suburbs would never survive long enough to boast of having one day. They were built for impermanence. Yes, it must have been a special occasion. My parents usually took us out to dinner for Chinese or steak sandwiches up the street, stopping at the custard stand for dessert. Blue Bell was thirty minutes away, in an unknown world.

"Reservations for four," my father had said. The hostess led us to our table. The restaurant was quiet, even though it was full.

"Get a load of this," my mother said. She had a smear of lipstick on her front tooth. "In a fancy restaurant. So elegant."

Her costume jewelry jangled as her arm extended downward to indicate the wall-to-wall carpeting, which seemed black but on closer inspection was a dark red with tiny blue shapes dotted through it like spying eyes. I was nervous. The Copper Kettle, hushed and dimly lit, was going to be one of those on-your-best-behavior places. I glanced at Adrienne; she was busy surveying the room, on the prowl for cute guys no doubt.

All of us ordered the house specialty: steak soup. When it arrived, my mother wrapped her fingers around the handle on the side of her bowl. "*Oy*. Bowls with a *shmetzl*."

I grabbed my handle. She was right. It felt like my pecker did when I woke up in the mornings, except bigger and more bulbous at the tip. The kind I hoped to have one day.

"Henry, napkin on lap please." It was cloth, with many perfect pleats.

I stirred the soup. It wasn't much different from the canned beef barley soup my mother served for lunch on weekends, only the pieces of meat were bigger and not compressed into perfect cubes like the ones out of the cans. The broth had the same orange color but wasn't as watery.

"So thick and hearty," she said.

"It's the flour," I told her. I learned the power of flour from the papier mâché project for Social Studies she and my dad helped me with the year before. He supplied the chicken wire for the bust of George Washington I was going to make, and she helped me tear newspaper into long strips that I was to dip into the flour–water concoction she'd mixed together in a large plastic bowl and slap them against chicken wire until it turned into George Washington. The strips kept slipping down the chicken wire. I got a C. My first.

"They wouldn't use flour in this kind of place," she said. "It's a beef stock reduction. Probably with a pinch of agar-agar."

I had no idea what she was talking about. I brought a spoonful to my mouth.

"It's hot," she said. "Careful not to slurp like you do at home."

The reunion to be held at the Copper Kettle Inn was organized by Gretchen (aka "the Retch") Dufresne (nee Schwartz). Leave it to her. At school, she signed up for the extra-curricular activities that had little if anything to do with beauty or intelligence, neither of which she possessed to a noticeable degree. Activities like "Home Gardening Club," "Ars Medica," and "Pen Pal Club." Thirty years later she was still at it. Some things didn't change.

I wondered how unchanged I was after thirty years. I still took quick showers, but after the invitation to the reunion arrived, I lingered in front of the mirror above the sink, where I practiced variations on a full smile and beaming eyes. If I worked those gestures properly, I'd be able to outsmart the harsher edges of my aging—the receding hairline, the graying temples, the sallow cheeks and crevicing geography of my face—and build confidence when I was face to face with my classmates, many of whom had been indifferent to me for reasons I hadn't understood at the time. I'd carry on this way in front of the mirror until I lost any ability to see who I was, who I'd been, what version of me I was hoping to pass myself off as.

I wondered about Donny too, what all the years might have turned him into and whether I really wanted to find out or whether I preferred to hold on to my version of him. Regardless of the choice, was it necessary to subject myself to the salivating jowls of our past snapping at the heels of my present, determined to nab me, drag me off and devour me all over again? I wiped the residual steam off the mirror. The reunion boiled down to Donny, who might not even be there. Then what? And even worse, what if he was there? Then what?

"I think I won't go," I told Len.

"Let's go together. It'll be fun."

"Fun? For you maybe. What would you like to come as?

My spokesperson? My shrink?"

He took a few steps toward me but left enough space that another person could fit into. "Ease up," he said. "It was only a suggestion. No big deal."

He was right, as usual. It shouldn't be a big deal. But Donny was a big deal, a fixed condition of mine that flared up unexpectedly like asthma. "Let's say I go and you come with me. What'll I call you?" Eighteen years together and I still hadn't figured out how to introduce Len to those who hadn't seen us together enough to figure it out for themselves. A simple "This is Len" would have worked, except he had the habit of holding my hand or nuzzling me in public. I couldn't bring myself to ask him not to touch me at the reunion. It would have caused an overwrought discussion between us that I didn't deserve to win. The alternative was to pinpoint some single word to label us and then leave it up to the others to react to. Spouse was militant; partner was business-like; significant-other was Hallmark; better-half was denigrating; mate was derivative. If he came with me, I'd have to call him something. On the other hand, if I didn't bring him with me, I'd have to explain why I was alone. If I didn't go at all, I wouldn't have to explain anything to anyone.

"How about 'This is Len, my husband,'" he said as he took one step closer.

"To the Spring Valley Class of '75? Are you out of your mind?"

"You don't think some of them might have changed?"

He had a point. Thirty years is a long time to stay the same about matters of the heart, especially after all the heartache that comes with the deal. I flashed on two classmates of mine, Janice Cooke and Billy Waldman. There was nothing exceptional about them either, until she got pregnant by him at the beginning of our senior year and they got married the following summer. In the hallways, they seemed happy and calm. Were they still together? I hoped so.

I checked the reunion website each day, scrolling through the vintage snapshots that were streaming in—classmates clustered in the cliques I was excluded from, classmate couples going steady, individual classmates in their moment of glory as they dunked a basketball, did a split, faced the principal at the podium during assembly as he handed them a scrolled certificate of excellence—and a few photos that were taken more recently, mostly of the popular girls who were eager to display their long glossy hair cascading over their shoulders and ending at the cleavage, whose vee was still as pronounced and proud as soaring birds in chevron flight. Those girls. They all looked the same to me then and as they did now, as unfair as that might be. I was searching for something else. Into my second hour in front of the computer after I'd seen Toby off to bed, I heard soft footsteps behind me that stopped as soon as a hand landed gently on my shoulder.

"What are you looking at?" Len asked me.

"Photos on the reunion website."

He rested his chin on top of my head. "Do you recognize them?"

"The women, mostly. They work harder to look like they did three decades ago."

"You think so?" He kissed my temple. "And what are you looking for? Did you find him?"

"Who?"

"Is his hair still red? Maybe he doesn't have much hair. Even less than you. Maybe he's pear-shaped. Even more than you." His hand traveled to my waist and squeezed my spare tire.

"Am I pear-shaped?"

He squeezed it again. "To bed with you. It's late."

"You sound like my mother." I rose from the chair.

"I usually liked your mother. It was easy to. Probably because she wasn't my mother. Now come. It's late. It's chilly. I need you spooned up against me. You can be on the inside this time." He removed his hand from my waist and I was adrift.

"You can try to find him tomorrow."

"What if he isn't there?"

"What if he is?" He tousled my hair, a habit of his that he took pleasure in doing, especially at the sides above my temples where the hair went haywire. "Does it matter? Either way?" He pulled my face close to his. "Let's go, Reds."

We lay down in our bed. "Make a letter C," he instructed me. "I'll mold myself behind you from my side."

I did as he told me and went further, curving myself into a lower-case O so that more of him could fit around me. I lay there wrapped inside him until he started snoring, which usually took only a minute or two. As I eased myself out from the shelter of him, he rolled onto his back and reached over to the night table to get his nasal spray.

"Sorry," he said. "You know I saw wood at night. I can't help it."

"You're forgiven. After all, I fart whenever I shift from my side to my stomach."

He injected the nasal spray nozzle into the problematic nostril. "You think I don't know that? I have a quick remedy for my little disturbance." He gave the base of the spray a quick squeeze, turned toward me and slid his hands down to my buttocks. "What about you?"

"No such cure. What can I say? I'm a li'l stinker."

He kissed me on the tip of my nose before rolling onto his other side, away from me. "Good night." His right arm traveled behind him to the space between us, grazing against me to make sure I was still there. "Listen carefully."

"To what?"

"Listen."

"Okay."

"Ready?"

"Ready for what?"

"For this." He broke wind.

As I curled myself around him, I resolved to not look for

snapshots of Donny the next day. My version of Len worked much better almost all of the time; on the occasions when it didn't, I wasn't overly unsettled.

I pressed myself closer, not so close as to wake him up, but just enough to ignite the collective body heat I needed to induce me into the deep sleep that Len was able to enter into each night without effort. Oh, to fall asleep like that, especially tonight. It was a Friday and Toby would wake up in the morning before either of us did, dash into our bedroom unannounced and wiggle himself between our tightness. There'd be room.

I MADE SURE OUR outfits for the reunion had nothing to do with complementarity. That our clothes shared the same closet and chest of drawers was nobody's business. I chose a pair of khakis and a loose-fitting linen jacket. Len agreed to wear a dark-blue fitted suit. He held out a red bowtie. I bristled.

"Let me guess," he said. "Too gay." He put it up to his collar. "Or too red." He sounded uncharacteristically annoyed.

I pulled a red necktie from the tie rack. "Compromise?"

"Of course," he said. "Where would we be if we didn't give each other some slack?"

Slack indeed. I stood behind him and tied the Windsor knot that I was in the habit of tying for him whenever he gave in to wearing a necktie; only on this occasion I pulled it tighter than usual.

"See that ship in a bottle up there on the top shelf?" I asked him as we were approaching the check-in table in the foyer of the Copper Kettle Inn. "It was there on that shelf when I was a kid. I asked my father how they got it inside the bottle."

"What did your father say?"

"He said, 'Don't dawdle. Follow the hostess to the table.'"

"Not convinced," Len replied.

"Why don't you tell me then. What did my father say?"

"I wasn't there," he said. "You were, but you were a pint-size version of you. You probably can't remember all that well."

"Then why the hell did you ask me?"

He stroked my cheek. "To see if you could admit to not remembering something."

"They may not have been my father's exact words, but one thing he didn't tell me was how they got the ship inside the bottle. Are you satisfied?"

"Do I have a choice?" He kissed my cheek.

"I do remember feeling sad when I saw such a beautiful and intricate object trapped inside that glass cage."

Len kissed my other cheek.

The check-in table was decked out with thick magic markers and sheets of adhesive name tags.

"Help yourself to a marker," the women behind the counter told us. "Write your name on a tag and stick it on your jacket where everyone can see it." I checked out her name tag when she wasn't looking.

"Gretchen!" I said to her.

"How did you know?"

I told her what all of us wanted to hear. "You haven't changed a bit."

"You're very wrong about that, but thank you."

"I'm Henry."

She paused. "Hmmm. Doesn't ring a bell. You must've been in a different section, Henry. Anyways, I'm glad you could make it. Have fun!"

Len and I filled out our name tags. "You didn't introduce me to her," he said.

"You could've introduced yourself."

"You didn't know who she was, did you?"

"Never saw her before in my life."

The reception room was full. The dozen or so chairs around each of the large tables were mostly empty as people milled about, drinks in hand, squinting from time to time at a name tag to see if the classmate it was attached to was worth stopping to have a chat with. Lots of women with too much make-up and tortured hair. Lots of men with bloated bellies and shiny pates.

"Do you see him?" Len asked.

"You'll be the first to know. Chill out. Let's go to the hors d'oeuvres," I said. "Down at the end, where the cocktail glasses are laid out."

Len helped himself to the self-serve sangria, letting the ladle skim the surface of the huge bowl so that he could scoop up a mass of fruit slices and ice cubes. I took a glass of red wine from among the neat rows of pre-filled plastic goblets.

"Do you want to grab something substantial to eat at the other end of the table?" he asked.

"No. I'm more comfortable near the alcohol zone."

There we stood, surveying the room like two lighthouses monitoring atmospheric conditions.

"So who do you recognize?" he asked.

"A few people, I think, but no one I ever spoke to in school, so there's no reason to speak to them now." I pointed to a woman not too far from us who was reaching for a breaded hors d'oeuvre shaped like a finger. I whispered close to his ear, "That's Randee Levine. Junior varsity cheerleader until she went all hippie. Tie-dye, macrame, headbands. The whole package. She was known for her big boobs. More so once she stopped wearing a bra. One time, when she was in her hippie mode, she saw me in the library stacks and asked me if I wanted to feel her up."

"Did you?"

"I wanted to, but I didn't."

"Why not?" he asked.

"I was afraid I wouldn't like it. And I wasn't ready for that."

Len stirred his sangria with a finger. "You could always go up to her now and remind her of your unfinished business."

He put his finger in his mouth to wipe off the excess.

I scanned the room again. "There are patterns taking shape," I said.

"Patterns?"

"Clusters." I revised myself again. "Cliques. The same old ones." I pointed toward a potted tree in the middle of the room. "See the tall overweight guy there with the red frizzy hair?"

"Don't tell me that's..."

"Please. That onion-shaped and onion-colored guy? No it's not. Once upon a time that guy was our star quarterback and Homecoming King. Larry Something. Or Harry Something."

"How about Gary Something?"

"No," I said. "It had two Rs. Don't ask me why I know that. All those guys swarming around him were part of the jock clique. Hard to believe, looking at them now."

"How do you know for sure?"

"Len, gimme a break. Who else could they be? National Merit Scholarship winners?"

He dipped his thumb and index finger into his glass, tweezed out a wedge of orange, gnawed on it, and deposited the peel back into the glass. "Right. The law of attraction. History repeating itself. The road most traveled. Something along those lines."

I downed my wine in a few gulps. "Skimpy portions."

The bartender was lolling behind the table, waiting to refill the bowl of sangria or lay out more plastic goblets and fill them halfway from the large bottles of red and white wine on the table. No other alcohol was being offered, and there was nothing else for him to do to occupy his time. Poor guy. I felt sorry for him, wanted to console him—perhaps as a first step toward seduction—even though he could have been the restaurant owner for all I knew. I couldn't find the elements of attraction that usually drew me into play. His body language was mute, his movements lumbering, as he maneuvered wearily in the cramped space allocated to him behind the fold-out table. He seemed spent. Still, I couldn't take my eyes off him. He was wearing our high school graduation ring, although I couldn't make out the year. Why was he stuck behind the beverage area in that white apron and ridiculous puffy paper chef hat?

"Excuse me," I said, "could you fill my glass?"

He picked up the bottle of red wine with his left hand and poured, stopping at the halfway point as he'd done with all of the glasses lined up on the table.

"You can fill it all the way," I said. "Unless it's against the rules." He continued pouring until the goblet was full and then set the bottle back on the table. No wedding band. Dirt under some of his fingernails. A three-letter initial ring: DOA. "Thanks very much." He didn't respond. "I appreciate it," I added.

"You're welcome," he said.

I knew it was him. I stood there sipping my wine, waiting for one of us to say something. I knew it would have to be me.

"Do you still play tetherball?" I asked.

"Not really."

"We used to have fun playing that. Hours and hours."

"I guess so," he said without looking at me. "It was kind of a stupid game though." He turned and pushed through the swinging doors to the service area.

"Yeah, I guess so," I replied well after he could have heard me. I lifted my glass to have yet another sip of wine. The glass was empty.

Len poked my elbow. "Henry to Earth. Let's circulate," he said.

"Do we have to?"

"*We* don't have to. But *you* should. It's your reunion. You've been standing here all this time. Go. I'll hang here and wait for you. Don't take too long, though. I might drink too much."

As I made my way through the room, I felt an affinity with the man who'd filled my glass: a kindred spirit who needed to be left alone in his insignificance. Wish granted. No one who squinted their eyes to read my name tag as I passed approached me. I looped back to Len after twenty minutes.

"Let's go," I said when I arrived at his side. "Did you grab some food?"

"No. I've been here all the time. So? What scandals did you unearth?"

"Nothing. I didn't speak to anyone."

He tipped his glass to slide the last ice cube into his mouth. "You've disappointed me. I expected some gossip. It brings out the catty side of you, which is fun." I didn't smile. "If you want, we can go."

"I want, please. Let's go." He took my hand and made for the exit.

There wasn't a soul in the parking lot. I looked at my watch. No wonder. Seven o'clock was too late for anyone to be arriving and too early for anyone to be leaving. I insisted on driving. "You had more to drink than I did," I said.

"Do you want to stop somewhere and grab a bite to eat?"

"Let's just head home."

The windshield wipers removed most of the gathering frost in one swing. Len turned on the heat to melt the remaining bits.

"Let's not take the Expressway if you're not in a hurry," he said. "I'm in the mood for the back roads. It's a nice night." I didn't mind the longer drive, the quieter drive, the silence broken only by the drubbing of the windshield wipers, a comforting collective heartbeat of Len, me, and the vehicle that would take us home. Len and me tooling around in our car. Its rusting roof and the stain on the console from when baby Toby threw up his strained beets were like already being home.

"What were you up to while I was milling about not saying anything to anyone?" I asked him as we were approaching the sprawling stone and gabled mansion we loved to fantasize about owning one day. The automatic sensor lights above the

front door were activated, showcasing the semicircular driveway and the sculpted shrubbery in the yard that Len always
commented resembled Disney World. Len could be catty too.

"I helped myself to another sangria. Probably more than
one," he said. "The bartender came back to replenish the bowl
and I tried to pick up where you left off. Didn't get very far."

"He seemed so resigned behind the table. Like a caged
animal."

"Maybe he wasn't the talkative type." Len turned off the
heat and cracked open his window to let in a slice of chill
autumn air. "That's better," he said. "You don't mind, do you?"
He didn't wait for me to answer. "He did tell me he was passing through when I asked him if he lived here. On his way to
West Virginia. He didn't say where he was coming from. But I
didn't ask him where he was coming from."

"What else?"

"I asked him how he ended up tending bar for the reunion.
He said he used to live here a while ago."

"And?"

"That's it. I stopped there." He switched on the radio. "I
didn't want to bother him any more." He lowered the volume
on the radio and turned toward me. "Not quite the Donny
you were expecting." He reached over and took my hand. "I'm
sorry for that, Henry." If Len's hand hadn't bent and curved
around mine to make a perfect fit, I might have felt sorry too.
But I didn't. Sad, perhaps. The type of sadness that can hurt
more than any physical pain I'd experienced. But not sorry.

When we arrived home, Len closed the front door behind
us and loosened his tie until the Windsor knot rested against
his breastbone. "Are you glad you went?"

"I'm gladder it's over and done with." The wall hooks were
full. I draped my jacket over Len's baseball cap and pressed
on it so it wouldn't slip off. "It's nice to be home." I turned
around and went limp in his arms.

He stroked the back of my neck the way I had come to

expect, rubbing his cupped hand up and down both sides and occasionally extending his index finger to locate a node that he would then push into to make me flinch with pain followed by an "ahhh" of relief. For years, he'd explored and discovered the terrain of my neck—and other zones of my pain and relief—as no one else could.

"I love us," he said.

"You're drunk."

"So I am," he admitted.

I grabbed the ends of his tie and pulled them above his head until the loosened loop of the tie resembled a dangling noose about to be tightened. "I could put an end to you right now," I said.

"So you could. But you won't. You love us too."

I let the tie drop. The loop caught on his left ear. I unhooked it, unbuttoned the top button of his shirt, and slipped my hand inside to feel his chest in the way that I did when I wanted to let him know how much I loved him without telling him so. "Let's check on Toby," I said.

We made our way down the hallway, past the bathroom and linen closet doors to Toby's room. His door was open; the room empty. We hurried to our bedroom. There he was: fast asleep, belly up, arms splayed like a cross, head on Len's pillow, feet at the bottom of my side of the mattress, the blanket and top sheet pushed to the floor at the foot of the bed. The distal edges of his toenails were long and grimy, the bottoms of his feet solid black. Filthy, stinky boy. Lovely boy. Our child.

"He's claimed our hallowed space for tonight," Len whispered.

"You reckon?" I stripped down to my T-shirt and boxers, leaving my outer attire in a heap on the floor, and gently eked out a wedge of mattress on my side of the bed without waking Toby. "Your turn," I said. "Strip down to your undies and work yourself in."

He looked at the queen-size mattress as he peeled off his clothes.

"Atta boy," I said. "There's more than enough room for all of us."

TOBY STOPPED BARGING in on our weekend morning sleep-ins after he learned how to read on his own. He'd sit quietly in his room with a book, and Len or I would be the one to do the barging. He or I would crack open his bedroom door and say in a soft morning voice, "Toby, come down for breakfast."

As soon as he got his learner's permit, he was out of the house before Len and I woke up. We knew where to find him: in our car, going up and down the driveway. At about the same time, he started taking showers every day and avoiding physical contact with Len or me.

"Do you think he's having sex?" I asked Len.

"Probably," he said.

"With a girl? A boy?"

"Doesn't matter. He's caught the whiff of sex and he's hooked. Surprise surprise. I only hope he uses a condom and his grades don't plummet."

"I found a washcloth under his bed the other day. It had stiff yellow blotches on it."

"There you go," he said. "Classic. I used a sock. I kept it in the back of the bottom drawer of my chest of drawers. My mom still managed to find it."

"What did she say to you?" I asked him.

"She didn't say anything," he said. "One morning when I went to use it, it wasn't there. I found it in my sock drawer, all clean and paired with its missing other half."

"What do you use now?"

"Besides you? None of your business."

"So I shouldn't say anything to Toby? I should mind my own business?"

"We should be safe," he said. "I found a small box of condoms in his night table drawer."

"Why didn't you tell me?"

"Because it wasn't opened yet."

Apparently Toby liked girls. The first one was named Jessica. He brought her home one afternoon after school.

"She's going to help me with my trig," he said as they whizzed by me to his bedroom. I heard the lock on his door click.

"Let me know if you need anything," I called out. No answer. I took the package of Chips Ahoy! from the pantry and a dish from the kitchen cabinet. My idea was to layer the cookies in a spiral around the dish, like fallen dominoes. After arranging the first three I returned two of them to the package, ate the remaining one, brushed off the dish and put it and the package of cookies away. They could be deep in their studies. Or fucking. Cookies? Who was I kidding?

Jessica was short-lived. Next came Donna. Her hair was long and bleached blonde, ending in sickly strands a few inches below her long neck. Her mousy brown roots formed a thin stripe along her center part. When he brought her home, she said, "It's so nice to meet you. I've heard so much about you."

"Is that so? Like what? Tell me about me," I wanted to say. Instead, I smiled and waited to hear the click of Toby's bedroom door lock.

A few others came through the front door. Their names escape me, if I was ever formally introduced to them. They were short-lived too. There was so much to ask him and talk to him about. I kept quiet. The animal smell that pervaded his bedroom and a stock of condoms I discovered in the left shoe of the wing tips he rarely wore were as much as I needed to experience. I wasn't mattering to him as much as I used to, which I'd have to get used to. I decided to let him call the shots. He didn't call any, except once when he thought he had crabs and asked me to inspect his pubic hairs. I saw movement in his bush, recommended Kwell, and took him to the pharmacy. "Do you want me to wait in the car?" I asked him.

"Would you mind coming with me?"

"If you want." As we crossed the parking lot, he took my arm.

"Thanks, Dad."

I smiled and wondered how much of me he would hold onto as he was letting go of me.

TOBY'S DORM ROOM in Vermont was miniscule. Len and I drove him there. "I don't mind doing the driving," I told Len as we were loading up the trunk.

"That's okay. I can drive," he said. "You'll spend too much time gawking at Toby in the rearview mirror. I want us to get there in one piece."

"Three pieces," I said.

"One piece," he repeated.

As soon as Len turned the ignition, WIGB was blaring rapid-fire rap through the four speakers of the car. It could be Eminem, but what did I know? It sounded like something that would resonate with Toby and therefore made me feel old. I looked over my shoulder to see his reaction to the music. He was already wired to his MP3, eyes closed, head bobbing, far away from anything we might have to offer. Oh, to yank the buds from his ears. Can't you wait until we arrive to tune us out? Are six more hours so much to ask for?

"Len, can you switch the station or lower the volume?"

At intervals, I turned around to Toby, gestured to him to remove his earbuds, and asked him if he wouldn't mind making a stop. Most of the route was off the main highway. Placards announced exits for towns I hadn't been to but had a certain caché—New Paltz, Saratoga Springs—and towns I'd never heard of but whose names were suggestive—Saugerties, Coxsackie. Anything to remain en route to the final destination where we'd have to deposit Toby and his belongings, turn the car around, and head home with the back seat empty.

"Nah. Let's keep going," Toby said. I didn't push it more than two or three times. I didn't push anything too much with Toby. One glance from Len, bless his soul, was all it took for me to back off. Our only stop was at a Cracker Barrel for lunch. We played Tricky Triangle while we waited for our food. When the server brought us lunch—three meatloaf platters (Toby ordered first, and we followed suit, as if in a final act of solidarity)—we continued the game while we ate.

Back on the highway, static infiltrated WIGB and soon obliterated the radio station altogether. Len pressed the automatic scan button—commercials, dentist office music, or a song that seemed promising until the word "Jesus" cropped up and dominated the airwaves. "Why don't you choose a CD from the glove compartment," he said.

I pushed the lever and the glove compartment drawer snapped open. Joni Mitchell was on top of the stack. Perfect. She deserved to be on top forever. Screw rap! I inserted the disk and waited for the opening word that for decades had the effect of instantly soothing my aching soul: Blue. A warm color, a melancholy mood, all compressed into one syllable that Joni was audacious enough to draw out through seven beats and seven notes to make its breadth and depth felt down to the marrow. Blue. She knew a thing or two. I wondered if Toby had even heard of her.

Once we hit upstate New York, the silence among the three of us was less disquieting. The unending expanse of deciduous and coniferous hills made the situation of three people packed tightly into an automobile and not talking to each other seem irrelevant. We occupied ourselves in our separate silences for the next three hours, interrupted occasionally by Len coughing.

"What's with the cough?" I asked him. "Are you coming down with something?"

"Nah," he said. "I'm perfectly fine. Probably some allergy I never knew I had. Different vegetation in these parts. Weird pollen."

We arrived at the Middlebury campus early, a noble enclave of stone and buildings cloaked in carefully tended greenery, as I'd expected, considering its reputation and the associated financial outlay. The sense of privilege and exclusivity made me queasy and a little guilty until we entered Toby's dorm room, which he was to share with another student. The room was spartan. A less-than-single bed, small desk and chest of drawers to the left, mirrored on the right with its doppelganger. The one window was the size of the laminated list of room regulations framed on the door. A prison cell. I was horrified. Len shrugged his shoulders. Toby was unperturbed.

"I told you we packed too much, Dad," he said to me.

"So you did," Len said. "Take what you want. We can drive the rest home." He glanced around the room.

I looked at the bed and tried to imagine how Toby would be able to play out a relationship in a substantial way. Impossible in this space, in that bed, on that thin mattress. Would he even bother to use the new sets of sheets we'd bought for him?

Toby moved briskly to extract a few boxes and duffel bags from the trunk. I couldn't make any sense of his choices. He seemed decisive and indifferent at the same time.

"That should do it," he said as he closed the trunk, still two-thirds full.

"But look at the..."

Len interrupted me. "Let us know if you need anything else." It was clear to me that Toby didn't have a clue as to what he needed, except to have us leave as soon as possible and get on with the business of having his very own life. Len nudged me toward the driver's side of the car. "I guess it's time we head off."

"Yep," Toby said.

They were conspiring against me. Why was I so resistant to understanding what the two of them were understanding so easily?

Toby walked toward me, arms outstretched. He was familiar with my bouts of agitation. Nevertheless, his hug was weak, and started loosening before he finished saying, "See you, Dad." He walked over to Len and hugged him. "See you, Pop." Their hug lingered beyond the three words. Len placed his lips near Toby's ear. Surely he was whispering a privacy to him. Yes, they were in cahoots. When they broke their embrace, Toby made an about-face and headed toward the dorm building without looking back. Perhaps that's what Len whispered to him: "Don't look back." He had a point. Len usually did.

Back on the highway, Len tapped my thigh, which caused my foot to press on the accelerator. "Take the next exit," he said. "And slow down."

"Our exit isn't for miles. Let's just get home."

"Home can wait a day. We're going to Saratoga Springs. I booked us a hotel suite." Len was onto me. Home might be the last place to be right now. "Let's treat ourselves to this," he said. "We've earned it."

"Earned what?"

"We can talk about it over dinner. For now, focus on driving. I'll let you know if I see anything out the window worth looking at."

The sun was well into its descent when we arrived at the hotel, which was once a private residence and now a historical landmark, according to the placard on the patch of front lawn. The gabled roof, brick façade, and Doric columns had been preserved; the three rows of windows had been upgraded to double-pane solid glass, each pane reflecting the pink waning light.

"Let's drop our bags in the room and walk around while the sun is still up and everything is open," Len said. "Stretch our legs."

We paused in front of the display windows of the many boutiques on the main drag, keeping an eye out for possible restaurants where we might eat, even though our hotel boasted a five-star restaurant. The commercial strip thinned after three blocks, but we continued until we noticed a run-down restaurant whose menu, posted on the front window, was fixed in lamination that had yellowed over time, like some amber-preserved fossil. The offerings were traditional, unencumbered by strings of descriptive adjectives.

"What do you think?" Len asked me.

"Perfect," I said. "Let's not turn dinner into an event. I've had my fill of events for today."

He stepped inside, made a reservation for seven o'clock, and we ambled back to the commercial strip to scrutinize more objects in display windows and invent reasons to not buy them. It was a game, one of several, that we played when we were alone together. Silly games that united us in laughter, in intimacy.

We did disagree on one object—a watercolor landscape centered in the large picture window of a gallery called "The Gallery." Len was tempted to buy it. "It's soothing," he said.

"So is aloe ointment," I said. He looked at his watch. Time to eat.

As the hostess was taking us toward a small round table in the middle of the dining room, I noticed an empty booth further back, near the kitchen and a corridor that probably led to the restrooms. "Is that booth down there available?" I asked.

"The round table here is fine," Len said to her. We sat down and ordered drinks. "Let's be in the thick of things tonight. It'll be quiet when we get home." He scanned one of the menus on the table and pointed to the oyster appetizer, which read "Oysters" followed by an asterisk. "Let's order a dozen to start." In the attenuated lighting, Len seemed younger. I hoped I did too. The last time we ordered oysters, they didn't have an asterisk with a caveat footnoted at the bottom of the menu. That was a long time ago. Was dying from eating an oyster a new development?

"Okay," I said. "Extra lemon and horseradish on the side for me."

"I haven't forgotten."

The server brought our drinks, two glasses of the house

pinot grigio. Len ordered the oysters. I raised my glass. "Here's to a long haul."

"Sure was," he said. "Six hours on the road, and two more toward home."

"Plus the seventeen years of child-rearing."

Len picked up his glass. "Ah, right. That too."

"Do you think he'll be okay?"

He smiled and took a sip of wine. "Absolutely not. How could he possibly live without us?" He took another sip. "Here's to our wonderful young man, our son. And to a very neurotic man, my husband. He'll be okay. Few have died from the condition of adolescence." He took a third sip and started coughing after he swallowed. When the coughing subsided, he asked, "How about you? Will *you* be okay?"

I took a second sip. "I don't know. A lot depends on whether *you'll* be okay."

The meal was decent. Its abundance enabled me to not talk much as I plowed my way through my thick slab of prime rib, which didn't seem to bother Len. I observed him eating his meal. He used his knife to help the food onto his fork. He bent over his plate to meet the fork. He clamped his teeth onto the fork as he was pulling it from his mouth, making a scraping noise. His usual idiosyncrasies. Sometimes they were endearing; other times annoying. On this night they were neither. They were simply Len, except when he wiped his mouth with his napkin after choking on a piece of prime rib. As he was crumpling the napkin before stuffing it into his pants pocket, I could make out red stains.

"The prime rib is really delicious," he said. "Super rare and bloody." He turned his eyes away from mine, sliced a piece of meat and brought it to my mouth, cupping his hand under the fork so that blood could gather there and corroborate. "Here, try some." The hand under his fork was dry.

We slept until ten o'clock the next morning. Unprecedented and shameful. Delicious. We might have slept even later if it hadn't been for light and heat pressing against my closed eyelids. When I opened my eyes, the morning sun, direct and harsh, had taken over the bedroom. We hadn't thought to draw the curtains. Curtains didn't register with us. Our bedroom windows at home didn't have them. The pine trees in front of the windows kept the morning light at a low level and muted it into a mellow green that resembled the color of a cabin deep in the woods.

Len drove the rest of the way home. For much of the trip we clasped hands on top of the console while we listened to the jazz stations I found on the radio. Between the soft music and our intertwined fingers, there wasn't a need for conversation. I still wasn't in the mood to talk, anyway. Len cleared his throat a lot, as if he were about to make a pronouncement, but he didn't say anything. He didn't expectorate blood either.

TOBY MET ALEXIS during the spring semester of his sophomore year. They shared the same cadaver in Anatomy 101, an elective course that he most likely chose to keep me quiet about the topic of career. I pressed him to be a doctor.

The first time they came to visit us, during spring break, Toby had a beard. "She asked me to grow one," he said. "It's pretty scraggly, but she doesn't seem to mind at all." Yes, the two of them are tight, but my most pressing concern was imagining him as a bearded doctor one day. Would I be able to locate him in all that change?

Each time they came to visit Len and me, they told us how they met while dissecting the cadaver, breaking into giggles when they admitted that they'd even given the cadaver a name: Reuben. I wondered why they kept telling us this story. Did they forget they'd told us before? Did they keep repeating it because they thought we were getting on in years and thus prone to forgetting? Did the telling of it give them a charge of connection that little else about their relationship was able to do except, perhaps, the beard he'd grown for her? Or the sex they had? I never asked them why. It was lovely to watch them giggle together.

I approved of Alexis. She called us Henry and Len from the get-go. She was pleasant to look at, without a surplus of beauty that can get in the way. No trace of make-up was to be found on her lightly freckled face, and her long brown hair thinned as it made its way down her back and ended with an uneven edge resembling a jagged line graph that didn't indicate a trend. One of her top front teeth overlapped the bottom edge of its neighboring tooth. She was perky and articulate when she spoke, even when I overheard her talking with Toby in private, and she made no effort to soften the rough edges of her Roxbury accent with its wide As and muted Rs. Most importantly, when all of us were together, she shared with my son a discernible code of gestures and words that reminded me of Len and me and the ease and mystery with which we fit together. They wouldn't change the world, as they probably thought they were destined to do at that age. But they demonstrated the promise of being able to eke out enough pleasure in the world and each other to make a successful go of it.

Alexis stayed the course of her studies and became a gastroenterologist; Toby jumped ship after the anatomy class and ended up in agroecology. The stuff of these two professions was a mystery to me, although the job titles were serious and impressive, even if they seemed galaxies apart. Toby and Alexis stayed the course of their relationship too and were married shortly after she started her internship. She kept her maiden name for a few months. Then she got pregnant, took Toby's hyphenated surname (our hyphenated surname) and redid her business cards. "It wasn't an accident," she told me. "We planned to start a family now." My eyes darted to Toby in time to see him shrug his shoulders so slightly that he probably wasn't even aware he was doing it. Alexis looked at him. He smiled.

In her fifth month, she suffered a miscarriage. Toby called me with the news while Alexis was coping with the betrayal of her body. He was a good son, a good husband. One day, he'd be a good father. After he stated the simple fact of their losing the baby, he said he needed to go and hoped that I'd understand. I responded with a simple, understandable lie—"Of course I do"—and gently cradled the phone onto its brace above the toaster oven. I was unable to move from the kitchen, which wasn't a new phenomenon. For some time, the rest of the house had taken on the aspect of a series of eerie echo chambers, what with Len dying almost a year before the announcement of the pregnancy. And now this, the baby dying too. How much of my imagined future in our spacious house could be erased by all this spectacularly unexpected absence? Who would be left to roam through all of the rooms and make themselves at home in this home besides me? *Beside* me?

LEN DYING. I was gently advised by his oncologist to expect it as soon as he was diagnosed with stage III lung cancer, although the doctor was at a loss for words as to how he got it to begin with. "I hear you," I said. "Of all places, those deep-breathing, nicotine-free lungs of his." From time to time, I recalled the incident of the blood on his napkin in the restaurant in Saratoga Springs after we'd dropped Toby off at the dorm and how, after the restaurant episode, he took up a new habit: clearing his throat regularly. It never lasted more than a second or two before he suppressed it by speaking, as if the throat-clearing was meant to be understood as a prelude to something important he was about to say and not his attempt to stifle a cough and the few drops of blood it might expel from his lungs and spew from his mouth. The next time I saw his blood coughed out was after he'd been admitted to the hospital for the last time and couldn't swallow the tapioca that the nurse had placed on his bed tray, even though he'd taken only one teaspoonful. I could have killed myself for not realizing the possible telltale sign in the restaurant. Len was a master when it came to not having anyone make a fuss over him.

I took some tissues from the side table and started to wipe up the thick traces of tapioca-blood from the bed tray. "Leave it," he said. "Hold my hand and be quiet. If you're quiet, I won't need to say anything either, which is a whole lot easier for me." His eyelids were at half-mast; he was struggling to hang on, as I'd been told to expect at this stage by one of the many hospital personnel who entered and exited his room.

"What if we...?"

"Shhhhhhh," he whispered. "Don't try to make sense out of this."

"What else can I do?"

He raised his left eyelid as if he were trying to lift a barbell. "Keep doing what you're doing. Holding my hand." He squeezed my hand with the energy he had in him before his grip would weaken, which it did. And just like that it was over.

Yes, the dying was expected, but not the actual death, which was a shock. I'd held his hand in the hospital bed many times before, each time wondering what it would be like if this time would end up being the last time. And this time was that time. His stomach no longer rose and fell with the simple rhythm that oxygen required to sustain a human organism; his flesh began to cool and stiffen to the touch; the skin on his face released the pain inscribed all over it moments ago—the pursed lips, crows' feet, clenched jaw, furrowed brow. He looked like a newborn, smooth and carefree, except that he wasn't entering the world. He had exited the world. In an instant and before my very eyes, he passed from being present to being absent. Totally. Forever.

I finished his cup of tapioca for him before pressing the call button hanging from the raised guardrail on the left side of his bed. What hurry was there? What could a nurse do to undo what had taken place? I hadn't eaten tapioca since I was a child. My mother served it regularly. She had a small shelf in the cupboard where she stacked the compact boxes of tapioca alongside the boxes of Jell-O. I loved Jell-O. It was fun. Tapioca wasn't. "Here you go. It's good for you. Sticks to your ribs," she used to tell me when she brought tapioca to the dinner table after clearing the plates to make room for the fancy dessert cups she'd poured it into before placing the cups in the fridge so the tapioca would set. She knew I didn't like tapioca. Whenever she decided I wouldn't like a particular food, she'd explain that it was good for me. If my reluctance persisted, she'd tack on the sticks-to-your-ribs phrase. She used it when serving oatmeal, canned creamed corn, and the dreaded liver *kreplach* with a drizzling of *schmaltz*. It was her way of saying, "Shut up and eat it."

The hospital tapioca tasted better than hers. I scraped the sides of the plastic cup to get every last bit. Maybe it was the dusting of cinnamon on top. My mother only used cinnamon for apple strudel. Or maybe it was an acquired taste that the adult version of me had arrived at after about half a century. Or maybe eating this tapioca simply gave me something to do until I figured out what to do next.

When there was nothing left except a few difficult-to-reach blobs below the lipped edge of the cup, I slid the cup to the side of the tray, looked at what was once my living Len, and pressed the call button. The nurse arrived holding her clipboard. Thank goodness it was Janelle, my favorite. Efficient and professional, and ready to lighten things up with a sassy remark. On one of my last visits to Len, I said to her, "He's complaining about being stiff."

She replied, "That sounds promising. Do you want me to come back later?"

She paused at the threshold of the room, looked at the bed and then at me. I waited for her to make a move, to say something. Surely she'd seen this a million times before and was an expert. It put an end to the private hope that a beloved was still in the process of dying and not yet dead.

She set her clipboard on the bedside table in order to take me around and hold me fully. I kept waiting for her to speak. All I heard was her breathing. And my breathing. I collapsed inside her embrace and started sobbing. She was a comfortable place to break down in.

"Cry, sweetheart. Don't hold back."

"I bet you say that to all the widowers."

She pulled away slowly and managed a smile. "I see that he finished his tapioca," she said. "God-awful stuff. At least it's sweet. No wonder Len liked it."

I didn't tell her that I'd eaten it. Janelle was so kind, so caring. She deserved to think that she knew Len, even if she got it wrong from time to time.

TOBY AND ALEXIS were in their late twenties when Len died too soon. They were going full-throttle with their ambition—for careers, social life, fitness regimes, progressive political causes, and then, as if that weren't enough, parenthood. They were unquenchable and unstoppable and perspired a lot. Tennis matches between them were fierce. They played like the lovers and archenemies that each was for the other. A solid couple. A driven couple, with plenty of time and range ahead of them to assume that everything they were reaching for, individually and collectively, would ultimately be graspable because they would have deserved it. How I envied their lubricated joints and their way of looking outward and upward, as if through a telescope, toward an outrageously accomplished future that they were confident they'd arrive at. Ad astrum. So fitting at that age. If not then, when?

They stopped by regularly to check on the new me: the me-minus-Len. Their visits were perfunctory, along the lines of:

"Hey, Dad, how are you doing today?"

"Okay, I guess."

"That's great."

Alexis chimes in. "Do you need anything?"

I don't know how to respond. The question is too vast. "Sure. Can you hand me my glasses on the side table over there?" Then they tell me about themselves and leave.

"Take care, Dad."

"Let us know if you need anything."

Hugs all around.

It was understandable that Len's death presented itself as an inconvenience to them, a bump in their momentum. They returned to the fullness of their lives, telescope out. And I returned to mine, paralyzed in the spot as soon as they released me from their hugs, with no idea of where to go and no clue as to why I should go anywhere. No matter. They couldn't have made my pain go away. And then the baby died and their own grief was born, as private and anarchic and unassailable as mine. But they were young and paired. I was neither.

Where did my telescope disappear to? Len would have known what to say to coax me away from the edge of my various precipices with his light touch. He'd have said, "Did you check behind the sofa?"

BOOK THREE

One

Lydia's hair is red and frizzy. Alexis became pregnant with her shortly after the miscarriage. She and Toby showed no trepidation over the news. In fact, they seemed emboldened by it. When Lydia was little and had her hair kept short like a skullcap, I called her "Matchstick," which made her giggle. By the time she stopped giggling about it, it was too late. The name had stuck.

The summer before she started junior high school, she decided to let her hair grow. Toby and Alexis didn't offer up any reservations. I objected.

"She'll look ridiculous with all that red frizz."

"It's Lydia's hair," they reminded me. "She has every right to own it." My son and daughter-in-law were in their late thirties.

"I've got news for you. No one owns anything." I was in my seventies.

Their eyes met and rolled for the one instant it takes couples to seal the deal on an act of collusion; they changed the subject to updates about the traffic and the weather. Typical. How I loathed when they diminished me in that way, as if my extra decades of living had somehow backfired, resulting in a deficit of insight and a cranky old man to be tolerated with kindness, notwithstanding those rolling eyes, until the visit was over. Len would have steered things in a different direction, I'm sure. But I was on my own and had been for a while, although not nearly long enough to get used to it, if that was possible.

After six months of growth, my granddaughter's head looked like a flaming pyramid set atop the thin pole of her neck. I was unquestionably right. She looked ridiculous. How could they not see it? How could Lydia not see it?

Apparently her hair was a hit at school. She told me that no one made fun of her, except for a couple of older jerks who tried to call her Reds but it had a shelf life of one miserable week.

"Lucky you," I told her. "I wasn't spared."

"I wouldn't have minded anyway," she said. "No big deal. You should hear what they called Marsha when she came to school with pink and purple streaks in her hair."

"What did they call her?"

"All-day sucker. Lucky for her it was spray dye. She rinsed it out when she got home from school, but the name stuck."

"Poor Marsha. I hope you didn't call her that."

"I didn't call her anything. She wasn't my friend. She wasn't anything. She was kind of creepy though." As she brushed a few strands of hair away from her chin, her thumb hooked her sweatshirt, pulling it to the left and exposing what looked like a bra strap. I gazed down to see if she had breasts. I couldn't make out any. "She needs to be noticed, but she doesn't have any friends. She's always alone in the halls and in the cafeteria."

"Maybe she hasn't found anyone to be friends with."

"Whatever. She's weird." She pushed her hair back again. "Maybe I'll get it trimmed. It gets in the way too much."

THREE HAIRSTYLES LATER, Lydia and her parents moved into my house. I gave it to them, reminding them that they didn't actually own it because I didn't own it. The bank owned a chunk of it and would continue to do so for the remainder of the twenty-year second mortgage Len and I took out after we inherited the house from my parents, moved into it, and immediately caught the fever of renovation. "We could go hog-wild in this place," Len said. "Let's hold to the essentials for now. New plumbing and electric. Solid and healthy bones. The rest in due course." In due course. A favorite expression of his. My father used it a lot too, compressing the three simple syllables into a single word, one that had the power to put an end to the discussion. I couldn't understand why my father didn't say "No" instead. Maybe he was experimenting with tact.

Len's "in due course" was different. He was literal, using the words to glide forward toward vague outcomes, not as a way to politely say, "Over my dead body." In this case, we did glide past the bones of the project of our house—first redoing the outdated hall bathroom with its baby pink and blue tiling, then the floor-to-ceiling Formica paneling in the family room, and on to the wall-to-wall carpeting in each of the bedrooms.

"Let's stop here," I said when he proposed a makeover of the half-bathroom off the family room. "The monthly payments are making me nervous."

"We can handle it," he said.

"Do we have to just because we can? Does it end?"

"God forbid it should end." He cleared his throat of the phlegm that had a habit of accumulating, but not of the volume required to produce the persistent cough that would later sound an alarm. "What would we do then? Kick back and wait for atrophy to set in?" From time to time he did cough. I attributed it to all the dust particles from the unending house projects. He probably had an allergy or two. Most people did.

After he died, the few rooms we'd fine-tuned left me indifferent. The others became oppressive. Too many to breathe life into and keep clean and fresh. Too much of everything for one person. How much does one person need?

"Take it," I told Toby. "You and Alexis need it. I don't anymore."

"But it's yours," Toby said.

"The bank might have a different idea about that," I replied. "I don't want it anymore."

"But..."

"Have at it. You'd be doing me a favor. You're going to inherit it anyway. Why not have it when you need it?"

Lydia grabbed me from behind and squeezed me. "Do we get to live here?"

"Ask your father."

"Can we, Dad?"

Toby looked at me. "Where would you go?"

"Somewhere nearby."

"Like?"

"Jesus, Toby. Are you expecting me to pull a spreadsheet of options from my back pocket? I'll look around and I'll find something."

As Lydia loosened her grip, I could feel against my back what were unmistakably breasts. "Can we live here, Dad? Can we?"

I waited for Toby to answer his daughter. He remained silent. So I stepped in.

"Grandpa says of course you can, my little matchstick. I promise I'll come visit."

She sped down the hall. "Mom, we get to live here!" By the time Lydia reached Alexis, they were out of hearing range.

Fifteen minutes before, Alexis had gone to lie down in the guest room at the far end of the hallway one split-level up. "I feel a migraine coming on," she said.

She'd never mentioned migraines before. I didn't believe her, but I didn't blame her for lying. No shame in needing some alone time. "Have a good rest," I said.

Toby's head was facing the window, although I could tell he wasn't gazing out so much as avoiding me. I could see it in his shoulders, taut and raised. I also noticed a few gray hairs threaded through his temples. If he'd had a beard, the gray hairs would have been even more prominent; that's where the gray hairs start to outnumber the brown ones. But my thirty-something-year-old son was now meticulous about being clean-shaven. He's getting older, although not old. He'll never be old to me. And I'll never be young to him.

"Let's get the bikes out of the garage and go for a ride," I said.

He stood up. "I'll pass if you don't mind. I'm tired."

"Why don't you lie down? I'll take Lydia."

"You must be tired too," he said.

"I'm not."

"I don't know how you do it," he said as he rose from his chair and headed down the hall to his wife and daughter.

"How I do what?" I asked.

"You know. Press on."

I wanted to tell him that I was too weary of everything in general to be tired of anything in particular. He wouldn't understand. Not at his age. "I'll get the bikes ready. Tell Lydia to meet me in the driveway."

A COUPLE OF months before Toby and Alexis moved into the house, I found a two-bedroom ranch house nearby on a cul-de-sac deep inside a 55+ subdivision. Maple Grove Pointe. I'd never noticed it before. The HOA rules and bylaws weren't as stringent as I'd expected. I didn't live in fear of being fined for having an unseemly splotch of mold on my roof shingles or weeds growing in my lawn. Thank goodness for that. What constituted a weed? Anything growing in your yard that you didn't plant yourself, even if it's pretty? Dogs of all sizes were permitted. Children visitors were allowed, even for long stretches. During holidays and summer breaks, the rumble of bicycles, skateboards and scooters from sunrise until sunset; the black asphalt festooned with cryptic love messages and hopscotch grids scrawled in chalk—pastel blue, pink and yellow—that washed away with the first decent rain. I listened to and gazed upon this activity of youth from my living room window. It gave me pleasure and I hoped it did the same for the neighbors who were watching. That's what elderly people do when they have nothing else to do. They stare out of the window, watching those who are absorbed in the life that they have. I wonder if the other window gazers are trying to extract pleasure from what they see and hear, or whether they're scavenging among a more deep-seated and mean-spirited reservoir—of envy, frustration, resentment, rage. How I fight that impulse when I watch young creatures darting about or blathering with energy and abandon. They have their whole lives ahead of them and can become anything, or so they believe. No reason to hold it against them.

The ultra-thin linen curtains I bought for the living room when I moved into my unit enabled me to watch them freely without being seen. I imagined stepping out of my house to a group of children chalking up the street and asking, "Can I play, too?" Surely they'd think me a senile old man, which is a shame because I'd have enjoyed playing. Could I still hop on one foot and make an about-face in mid-air in order to begin my return to the first block, stone in hand? As for the love notes, I wasn't as enthusiastic to join in. Who would I be writing to? And what would I have to say?

I bought colored chalk when I went to do the grocery shopping. The local supermarket carried boxes of Crayola Drawing Chalk in its modest Office Supplies section in Aisle 9. It would be nice to build the reputation of being the nice man who doles out chalk. The children could use the gesture as a baseline to invent their version of the rest of me, if they cared to take the trouble to do so, which I doubted they did.

I DIDN'T MISS the old house. It was one of many ghosts show-ing up in my new home like company. Ghosts on the prowl for a solid spot to drop anchor and begin the mission of coloniza-tion. Len was gliding around, of course. And my mother and father. Also Donny, although he mostly made his appearances in my night dreams, not my daydreams.

Toby and Alexis invited me to dinner, usually on Sundays, and turned out elaborate meals whose fragrances made my former kitchen an unrecognizable place. They picked me up and drove me home. I didn't reciprocate with dinner invita-tions. I'm sure they'd have accepted half the time. They kept tabs on such things, but it was possible that they were doing it in order to placate some part of me that they believed needed to be placated. Then I'd be offended and get all agitated and surly. Besides, Alexis was a wonderful cook. Then there was Lydia, rarely without her tiny white earbuds, even at the din-ner table. I didn't understand why she chose to be deaf to everything around her. She was too young to be blocking out so much of what was going on. Then again, I've never tried earbuds. Maybe I'm missing something. Her parents didn't seem to mind. Could be they preferred not hearing what she had to say.

"We're pretty sure she has a boyfriend," Toby told me over dinner one night when Lydia didn't appear at the table. "She's not home. Again."

Alexis dished out a portion of boeuf bourguignon that was enough for three meals. She knew I ate like a bird. "Help yourself to the noodles," she said. The wooden ladle she used had deep stains and fissures along the handle and bowl, so dif-ferent from the other immaculate table settings. It must have been my mother's. Certain minor household items have a way of not being discarded.

"There's no room on my plate for noodles. Nice plates, by the way."

"Sorry," she said. "I wasn't focusing." I took some noodles and placed them on top of the meat. "His name is Lowell," she continued. "I mean really. You can't get more wholesome than that. It begs delinquency."

"You're right," I replied. "With a name like that, Lowell is doomed to be a thug." I enjoyed yanking my daughter-in-law's chain.

"My point exactly. How can a kid who has to live with a name like that not think that he can get away with murder and then go about trying to prove he's right about it?"

"They called me Reds in school," I said. "The worst thing I did was shoplift a pack of Wrigley's spearmint gum with my friend Donny. He loved to get into mischief." I was about to add, "And I loved Donny," but instead stirred the noodles until they were distributed among the meat, pearl onions and sliced mushrooms. The meat was on the tough side. I was surprised. "Delicious," I told her. "Have you met this Lowell?"

"She's brought him home from school with her a few times."

"And?"

"He's polite. He looks me in the eyes when he asks me how I am. He has braces, the transparent kind, so he still smiles. He'll have nice teeth."

"That's sweet."

"No great feat on his part. We only spend about five seconds together before the two of them disappear."

Toby took a sip of wine. "Never met him. He's always gone by the time I get home from work."

I asked Alexis to pass me the bottle of wine.

"Already?" she asked.

"You didn't pour me any when we sat down."

"Oh dear, how could I have forgotten? That's a first. Sorry."

When she made no gesture toward the bottle, I reached

for it myself and filled my glass. "What's the big deal? It all sounds pretty normal to me." I looked first to Toby, who only shrugged his shoulders.

"Normal?" Alexis said. "Is it normal that I wonder whether I should offer them a plate of condoms instead of snacks before they run off?"

I took a gulp of wine. "I'm sure Lydia knows where you keep the snacks and the condoms. She can take what she needs all by herself." I took another gulp. "Alexis, would you rather that your daughter never brought a boy to the house? Or that she had nothing to do with boys altogether? Do you have some alternative in mind?"

"Screw you."

"Chill out, Alexis. She'll screw her way to the right man. You did. Toby did. I did too." I raised my glass in a gesture of coolness. She left the table. Toby shrugged his shoulders again and smiled.

Lowell and Lydia were together for two marking periods. Not a bad run. On the report cards during her debut romance, she got her first Bs—in Math and Social Studies—and her first C, in English of all things.

"A C in English?" I asked her after she'd broken up with Lowell and had more time for me. "You must have worked hard to be mediocre in English. Couldn't you have been mediocre in Home Ec.?"

"I cut English a lot," she confessed. "I had it last period. Lowell was in my class. He hated English. We'd meet down the hall before class and he'd convince me to sneak out of the building and make a mad dash across the baseball field to go to his house instead. Both his parents work. No one is home."

"Got it."

"Don't tell Mom and Dad."

"I won't if you tell me why you broke up and your As came back."

She lowered her head and let her hair pyramid swoop

down to cover her eyes and cheeks. "We got bored with each other. Like there were certain things we needed to get through and we found each other to get through them with, and after we got through them we couldn't come up with anything else that both of us wanted to do together."

"Got it. A dress rehearsal boyfriend. Smart cookie, you are."

"I guess. I hope so."

"I stand corrected. An *undressed* rehearsal boyfriend." I drew near her, pushed her hair back and looked into her eyes. "You know what I say to that?"

"What? No lectures. Please."

I worked my face into what I thought would radiate lightness and joy. "I say, 'Bring on the next!'" She laughed. "May there be many nexts." I rubbed my nose against hers. "Well, not too many."

She wrapped her arms around me. "Promise you won't tell Mom and Dad?"

"Now why would I tell them?"

She held me tighter. "You're so cool."

"That's me." She was a marvel to behold. Not that she was particularly beautiful. She was simply young and hungry for all that she didn't yet know, which made her intense and vibrant. How I envied her, warming up for her life and the boyfriends who would be her pit stops. The roller coaster of it all. I was ready to go home. My hip was acting up. I was tired. "Yep, so cool," I said as I got up to leave.

I MET MANY of my neighbors in Maple Grove Pointe when I took my morning and evening constitutionals along the edges of its sidewalk-less streets. It was like rummaging through a thrift store of human beings on display. Some of the residents were taking walks (with or without dogs), others were fine-tuning their front yards (with spades, rakes, shears, weed whackers), and others were seated on patio chairs in their open garages (with a drink in one hand and a glazed look). As a newcomer, I offered a simple smile to all, and a "hello" to most. As the weeks went by, I stopped those I'd seen more than a few times and attempted to enter into cordial conversation, especially with the walkers. Not as much with the tenders of yards. They seemed intent on their work, and I didn't want to disturb them. And never with the garage dwellers. People who perched themselves in their open garages to enjoy the great outdoors made me keep my head straight ahead. The bit of chit-chat I initiated with the walkers didn't pave the way to anything more. No one suggested an evening out, a game of golf, a visit to their back yard to select a few home-grown tomatoes or sprigs of dill or rosemary. Everyone seemed satisfied with a minute or two of light exchange. Except me. The constitutionals were pleasant enough as I was taking them, but once I returned home and closed the door behind me, an overwhelming sadness—sometimes verging on panic—seeped in. So many hours to still get through in the day and the night.

I did look forward to running into Eugene, the exception, a fit and attractive man with a full head of unruly white hair and a matching tuft of chest hair that cascaded from the polo shirts he wore like a uniform. I could see traces of where he'd attempted to make a part in his head hair, but the thick, straight mane had a mind of its own and the part was as jagged as a zipper. As much as I imagined how handsome he must have been when he was younger, I wasn't able to transpose the image to the present in order to get overly excited. Nevertheless, I enjoyed his company. He was around my age, a widower ("When my wife was alive," he'd said a few times), and had two children ("My son and daughter," he'd said a few times). When we stopped to chat the first time, I had my ice-breaker questions on the ready: "When did you move here?" "What did you do before you retired?" He answered dutifully and I expected him to ask the same of me. Instead, he asked, "*Why* did you move here?" "*Why* did you retire?" His questions reminded me of Toby during his "Why" period, which lasted until he started kindergarten. To every answer I gave my young son, he repeated the simple question—"Why?"—until I lost patience and said to him with a lack of gentleness that I regretted immediately afterward, "Okay, that's enough!" I felt guilty about this, but the further he dug down, the more difficult it was for me to answer him. If I let him continue long enough, he'd reach a place where I'd have to say, "I don't know," a confession that I was unwilling to admit to him, let alone to myself.

Eugene walked a Jack Russell that was nippy at first, but quickly gained my trust and tugged at his leash to arrive at my ankles as soon as he saw me on the street. His name was Jack, which took me a few encounters to remember—was it Russell or was it Jack? The name Eugene stuck the first time, one of those names that was standard enough—like Rudy or Ralph—but unlike Rudy or Ralph, I hadn't met anyone named Eugene until I met him, which made it memorable. Neither of us made a move to extend our friendship beyond our chance encounters on the street. I wasn't even sure which house was his, until I went to the end of my driveway one day to get the mail and found an invitation to his memorial service. Pale blue envelope, my name handwritten in the center, the return address in the left-hand corner. He lived on the next cul-de-sac over. The service was being held at his home, and I'd been invited somehow. I must have meant something to him too. How stupid of me to realize this after he was dead.

For the service, I chose my charcoal-gray suit with a pale blue Oxford cloth shirt and burgundy necktie. Neutral and inconspicuous for a gathering among strangers. Eugene's house was different than I'd imagined. It was extremely tidy. The wall-to-wall carpeting that came with every unit had been replaced by hardwood floors. Bookshelves were in abundance, the books with their spines aligned. Only two family photos were in evidence, one a traditional family portrait:

Eugene and the wife, with the two grown children behind them, hanging on a small wall next to the fireplace; the other a large framed and faded photo of a young sculler wearing a loose white sleeveless jersey with a deep purple "#3 Eugene" embossed across the chest. He was holding an oar and standing in front of a boat waiting for him at the river's edge. In the background, a boathouse. In the foreground, a beaming face with that same shock of hair, although the hair was black. I took a pre-poured glass of red wine and a celery stick filled with cream cheese and meandered through the attendees until I emptied my glass. I smiled a lot but said nothing. For the next few days after the memorial service, I found myself revising who I imagined Eugene was, in an effort to create the relationship that could have been.

IN THE FIVE years I lived in the Maple Grove Pointe house, Lydia stayed with me twice. The first time was when she was thirteen. Toby and Alexis were going to spend the weekend with friends in New York.

"Can you take her?" Alexis asked me. "We never get away."

"Of course I can," I said. "Alexis, don't you think she's old enough to stay home on her own if she wants to, and I'm sure she does?" Alexis looked at me as if I was out of my mind. I added, "Think back."

"Hey Grandpa," Lydia said when I opened the front door.

"Hi there. Who brought you?"

"Mom did. She was in a hurry so she dropped me off at the curb."

Her army-green backpack was large and its many zippered compartments were filled to the brim. How much did she need for a weekend with her grandfather? What was in there? She dropped the backpack on the floor with a thud.

"So what are we going to do?"

"You're not going to hide in the spare bedroom wishing you weren't here?"

She spent more time with me than I'd expected. Were Alexis or Toby behind it? Did one of them wave an admonishing index finger in front of her face and tell her to not hole up in the bedroom? Or did she enjoy my company? It was a crapshoot—what did I know about teenage girls? To cover my bases, I proposed cross-generational activities for Saturday: horseback riding on the Wissahickon bridle path, and a visit to the Rodin Museum downtown followed by dinner at a glass cube restaurant called Kweezeen. It went well. On Sunday, we let loose at the local specialty market. "One rule," I told her. "If you've eaten it before, you can't put it in the cart." Back home, we prepared a dinner of raw oysters, Dungeness crab legs, sauteed bok choy and a pint of Ben and Jerry's Funky Monkey. She set her Bose speaker on the counter and played her Pandora playlist for me while we prepped. From time to time I could discern the resemblance of a rhythm to a song, which helped me execute the chopping of the bok choy. At dinner, I showed her how to dislodge the oyster from the muscle that bound it to its shell, how to work the nutcracker and tiny fork to extract large chunks of meat from a crab claw. After dinner I accepted her offer to help me clean up, although I wouldn't have minded some quiet time above the sink and in front of the window looking out; she rinsed the dishes after soaking in the warm sink water and I arranged them in the dishwasher. The dishwasher came with the unit. I'd never used it. I hadn't used a dishwasher since Len died.

"Do you still have Parcheesi?" she asked, handing me the last of the dishes.

"I think I left it at my house—I mean your house—when I moved here."

"You left a bunch of stuff at the house. Who knows if Mom and Dad kept it?"

"You'll have to ask them," I said. "What else did I leave?"

She passed me the remaining utensils clenched in her hand like a bouquet. "A lot. Old textbooks, some paintings, your glass drawing board that you can make tilt up. I moved it into my room. I like it. It leaves lots of fingerprints though. Mom is always on my case about the fingerprints. She even left a roll of paper towels and a bottle of Windex next to my computer. But then she complains that I never empty my trash can when it's filled with wads of paper towel with my fingerprints on it. I mean really."

"You forgot something."

She swirled her hand in the residue of suds and food bits to feel around. "What? There's nothing here."

"No, not in the sink," I said. "At the house. A large item that I left. That my parents left me and that I left too."

"How would I know?"

"The big sofa. The L-shaped one." Before I closed the dishwasher door, my eyes traveled the strip of touch pads lining the top. "Would you mind turning on this contraption? I have no idea how this works. I'm used to a dial. Do you know what a dial is?"

She pressed the digital pad on the far right. "Some kind of soap, isn't it?"

I took her chin between my fingers.

"The sofa was yours?" she asked. "Mom and Dad sent it somewhere to be reupholstered when we moved in. I guess I forgot it was there before that. It's still pretty ugly. Why'd they bother anyway? They never use it."

"My mom and dad hardly used it either. Only when we had company, which was almost never." The dishwasher kicked in. I breathed in and out to the soft ticking of the timer. "I liked it though. If nothing else, it would be a great place to hide behind."

She reached for the dish towel hanging on the oven handle and dried her hands. "Did you ever hide behind it?"

"I might have once."

"Why?" She handed me the towel to do the same.

"Because I might have needed to." I replaced the damp

towel on the oven handle. "How about you? Did you ever?"

"No."

"Keep it in mind," I said. "It's a great place. Ugly as hell, though."

She gave me a peck on the cheek. "I'm going to my room now. There's decent wi-fi connection in there, right?"

"I've never tried to connect in that room. There should be." As she scurried off, I called out, "Let me know if there's a problem." Not that I could fix it if there was one. I heard the bedroom door slam. The day had been full. I was exhausted. She had other things to do.

THE SECOND TIME she stayed with me she was fifteen or sixteen. When I opened the front door, I found myself in front of a composite of resentment—glaring eyes, scowling face, stooped back and shoulders—so meticulous and studied that I wondered how long she'd worked at posturing herself before she rang the doorbell.

"Hey," was all she had to offer. She forgot to wipe her shoes on the welcome mat. Her clothes were tight and what my mother would call "whorey," her cobalt eyeliner thick and assertive, her bared left shoulder defaced with a tiny tattoo made up of three Arabic letters. And her gorgeous red hair was the color of squid ink, except for a two-inch band of red roots along the center part. Did she dye it a while ago and then change her mind? Or was the red band deliberate? Such a confusion of body markings and provocations, poor thing. Everything about her was begging for me to ask her what was wrong. It was clear what was wrong. At that age, everything was wrong.

I smiled at her. "Don't be so happy to see me."

"Sorry, Grandpa. I've got a lot on my mind."

"The mind is working. That's excellent news. Dump your stuff wherever and come in the kitchen. You must be hungry or thirsty."

"Both, actually."

She went to the refrigerator. "Do you have that peach iced tea?"

"Bottom shelf. Usual pitcher. I'll get the glass."

She found the pitcher and helped herself.

"Come. Sit." We sat down. She let herself cry.

I handed her a napkin. "I smell boy trouble."

"Partly right."

"The other part?"

"Mom trouble."

"Double whammy."

She poured herself some more iced tea. "They made me come here. That, or be grounded. You're my 'time-out,' gramps."

"For them or for you?" She managed a smile. "Which trouble should we talk about first?"

"Well, they're kind of connected. Mom caught me with my boyfriend, and I'm not even sure I want him as a boyfriend."

"Your mom'll get over it. It's part of her job description. Anger, empathy, forgiveness. Tell me, why aren't you sure?"

"Sure about what?"

"About your boyfriend. Can you give boyfriend a name, please?"

"Promise you won't laugh?"

"No guarantee."

She hesitated. "Clarence."

I laughed. "Poor guy. You can't even extrude a decent nickname from that."

She hesitated again. "Grandpa, do you think a guy who talks about himself all the time is not worth being in love with?"

"Did you ever try asking him to stop talking about himself and see what else he has to say?"

"I can't ask him to do that. He might want to break up with me."

"God forbid. Better to pretend to be happy in company than try to be happy alone. Seriously, though, he can't be talking about himself always. I mean, I don't think your mom caught the two of you in the act of him talking about himself."

"She caught us, you know, playing around."

"You didn't lock your bedroom door?"

"We weren't in my bedroom."

"Hmm." Lydia and Clarence behind the sofa. Alexis passing through the living room cradling a basket of clean laundry to distribute in their respective closets and chests of drawers. She sees a ribbon of white sticking out from under the sofa. As she tugs on it to realize it's the strap of her daughter's bra, she discerns two sets of legs behind the sofa. One pair is Lydia's. She recognizes the socks. The other set of legs is hairy. I love the image. I don't share it with her. "Your first time? Or your second if I haven't forgotten?"

"We didn't get that far." She was shaking. I was envious. When was the last time I shook over a guy?

"Were you hoping to?"

"I don't know."

I took the strand of hair dangling in front of her face and hooked it behind her ear. "Look at me," I said. In the few seconds it took for her to return my gaze, I realized I had nothing to say that could console her, if that was what she was after, and I doubted it was. I also doubted whether I should console her. Her suffering was pure. Why should I tamper with that?

Her eyes met mine. She waited for me to hold forth. "What?" she asked. Such angry eyes. Defying limits and, at the same time, pleading for limits. Pitch-perfect confusion.

"How about I fix us a bite to eat? What tickles your fancy?"

"Can we do oysters again?"

"Do you have some in your backpack? Otherwise we'll have to go out for dinner for them, which is fine by me. You decide."

She lowered her eyes. "Nah. It's fine here. You can make whatever."

Rummaging through the fridge, I could feel the heat of her eyes on me. "Would you settle for hot dogs and store-bought potato salad?"

"Sounds good," she said. "Can you put those diagonal lines in them with a knife and not boil them?"

I let my fingers graze the top of her head. "Okay, my little matchstick." How I wished the black dye would disappear. A small part of me wanted the entirety of her to disappear too, even if it meant her going back home and being grounded, poor thing. Be gone, Ms. Mope and Brood. Leave me alone. You try the patience of an old man like me. But a larger part of me wanted her to stay through the weekend. I was like her once, all obdurate and leaden and full of myself. So much silliness. So obnoxious. What vitality, what zest! What passion and promise! How to be led back to that place where every little thing had to be felt intensely because every little thing had to have meaning and shed light? My bones were growing dry and brittle, especially when I woke up in the morning or had to stoop down for whatever reason as the day pushed on. No denying it. And here was Lydia, highly combustible and itching to commit an act of arson. And here was me, the perfect tinder. No. I didn't want to be charred to a crisp in order to feed her flame. I wanted to be the flame, if only for a brief interval.

I took out a knife to make the diagonal slices in the hot dogs. "Go make yourself scarce," I said. "I'll call you when dinner is ready."

"Okay." She slung her backpack over her shoulder and disappeared while I pierced the skin of the hot dogs and made evenly spaced diagonal incisions before throwing them onto a cast iron griddle that I didn't remember having. It must have been my mother's, who also might have discovered it among her kitchenware when she was preparing a meal that

I'd requested and wondered where the griddle came from. Yet there it was, lodged below the non-stick skillet I used whenever I needed a pan. The discovery of the griddle, the surprising weight of it as I pulled it out, and the possibility of generational stories seared into its density of iron, gave me a sense of continuum that reassured me. Still. How did it get there?

Lydia complimented me on the hot dogs. "Wow, they taste like you made them on your barbecue," she said. I could have made them on the outdoor grill and spared myself the trouble of all those diagonal incisions. The problem was I didn't remember having an outdoor grill and wasn't convinced that I really had one. Curious. The small kitchen window facing the backyard only looked onto a patch of lawn and not the patio, where anyone with a bit of sense would situate a barbecue. Was there one out there within my property line? Would it have been a charcoal grill or one of those fancy gas ones? I had no idea.

"Next time I'll do them on the grill." I turned my gaze back to her and scrutinized her face. She was a mystery to me, but I recognized her. Lydia, my granddaughter. Lydia, my little matchstick. Lydia, the daughter of my son Toby, who had a wife, Alexis. I hammer their names into my head—Lydia. Toby. Alexis. I am a father, a grandfather, a widower. I am an ice floe whose time is coming. Solid chunks of me breaking off and floating away into the sea. Lydia mustn't float away. Lydia. Lydia. Lydia. I practiced the drill. She held fast. The fact of her name and of my curated reel of who she was remained intact. I was safe, for now anyway. I don't think she suspected that she, like the griddle and the grill and God knows what other pieces, was slipping away. That I was slipping away.

Two

After Eugene died and until I moved out of the Maple Grove Pointe subdivision, my constitutionals along the three streets and four cul-de-sacs each morning and late afternoon continued, weather permitting. I still looked forward to airing out and revisiting all the particulars I'd come to know so well. I counted on finding them in their places day after day, even if there were slight alterations in almost everything each day: Mrs. Stern's rhododendron bush pruned below the roof line; the D'Amatos' red convertible marred with a fresh dent on the back fender; vertical blinds installed above the Whites' picture window. It was important for me to take stock of these changes. They signified that my past and my present were on equal footing, that both tenses were holding firm. The details also kept me company, although I didn't make comments about them out loud or the neighbors might conclude I was loony-tunes as they edged their front yards or plowed their driveways or took out the garbage or were simply looking from a window to see for themselves the constants and the variables. Most of all, I looked forward to the possibility of running into another walker and exchanging a word or two, though I suspected that no one would captivate me like Eugene did. No one knew the neighborhood better than me.

I became disoriented twice that I can recall. The first time was during my first summer there, and I could have let it go had it not been for Lois, who stopped me abruptly on the street and asked, "Are you all right?"

"It's this heat wave," I told her. "I should've waited 'til later to have a stroll. I'm on my way home now."

She pointed in the other direction. "Your house is over there," she said.

"I know," I said. "I'm taking the scenic route."

"How about I walk with you?"

"That's okay," I said. She was a widow. No way was I going to open that door of need. "Thanks, though. I appreciate it, Lois." I emphasized her name to convince her that I had my wits about me. Or was her name Louise?

I must have got it right. She went on her way. "Enjoy your walk, Henry. Don't miss the Gallaghers' new mailbox on your way home. Done up like a birdhouse. That Rita is so creative."

"I'll make sure," I said. Who the hell was Rita? Who was she talking about? I proceeded down the street, squinting my eyes to blur the details of all the features that I usually took such pleasure in observing. I continued in this self-imposed haze for about a minute, and when I opened my eyes again, everything had returned to normal. I spotted my house two driveways away. Made it!

The second time was during my last winter at Maple Grove Pointe. A dusting of snow blew into the foyer when I opened the door to see who had rung the bell. It was Lydia. I hadn't seen her in a long time. She must have been eighteen or so. Her hair was short and restored to its natural red. She had a different backpack that wasn't clunky slung over her shoulder and a very tall boy beside her with his arm slung over her shoulders. Her arm was wrapped around his back and a gloved hand curled around his slender waist. I recognized her immediately.

"This is Josh," she said. "Do you mind?"

"Mind?"

"Us popping by."

Josh extended his free hand. "Pleasure to meet you, sir."

"Sir," I said. "I'm flattered." My intent was to make him blush. His cheeks were red, although it could have been from the bitter cold against his pale skin. Random strands of dirty blond hair dangled from under his wooly cap and petered out at his broad shoulders. "Don't stand there, you two. Come in."

Lydia led the way to the living room as if she were duchess of the manor and we the guests. I sat on the recliner at the far end of the room, leaving the three-seater sofa for the two of them to cuddle on until she could find it in her to spill about whatever troubles at home had brought her here while Josh held her tight; a collective force against the opposition—Toby and Alexis. Why else would she have called to ask if she could come over and bring this unknown boy? Lydia sat on one side and Josh on the other, each clutching an armrest as if for dear life. I saw a small stain on the middle seat cushion. Was that what was keeping them apart? "Remove stain, remove stain, remove stain," I said to myself so that after they'd gone I might not forget to write "Remove stain" on a Post-it and stick it on the refrigerator door with the other Post-its.

Lydia was thoughtful enough to take off her wet sneakers, although she brought her legs up and sat cross-legged, the heels of her feet against the fabric of the sofa. Her socks were filthy. The boy rested his head, without removing his damp headgear, against the wall. No Post-it required. The distance between them wasn't about the stain. It wasn't about them vs. Toby and Alexis either. It was about them. There they sat, restless and gloomy, looking at opposite sides of the room and saying nothing, waiting for me to say something, anything that would help them find their way back to each other. Looking to me, despite my age or because of it.

"So?" I asked.

After she told me she was pregnant, Josh produced a small blister pack from the inner breast pocket of his coat. "She wants to take this to get rid of the baby. I want to keep it."

"Keep it?" she asked. "Keep it? Is it yours to keep? That's news to me."

"You know what I mean."

"Oh yeah? Tell me everything I know about what you mean. Go for it."

"What does your mom have to say?" I asked her.

"She asked me what I plan to do and I told her I don't know. Then the phone rang and she took off to answer it like she always does. Some work issue she had to deal with. What else is new? When she hung up, she changed the subject while she went about her business. Never brought it up again. But every time she's around me her lips get razor-thin, like they could cut through flesh."

"And your dad?"

"He doesn't know anything. Not from me, anyway."

"You haven't told him?"

"No."

"Why not?"

"Mom'll tell him, if she hasn't already."

"So you didn't tell your dad, but you're telling me?"

"Because you won't freak out, Grandpa. You'll understand."

I tensed up. "Meaning I'll agree with you?" She lowered her eyes. I looked at the boy. "Sorry, what's your name again?"

"Josh, sir."

And then it happened. I looked at the young woman on my sofa almost in tears and had no idea who she was. Not her name, not her face. Not the red hair. Who were these two young people sitting in my living room? How did they get in here?

"Grandpa?" Lydia said. "Are you all right?"

I stood up. "I'm fine."

"Are you sure? You seem strange."

"Couldn't be better," I said. "I just need to lie down for a while. I usually do at this hour." I had no idea what time it was.

They rose from the sofa. The girl went first. The boy followed. I trailed behind to keep a safe distance. Where in this unfamiliar place was the front door? How did I get here? Did she call me Grandpa? When and how did that happen?

I closed the door behind them and did the eye-blurring thing. I made my way back to the sofa. In those few seconds, pieces started to reassemble into the familiar: Lydia and her red hair, the portrait on the wall of Len and me and our infant son Toby ("who grew up and married Alexis," I said to myself), the abacus lamp that I'd bought when I was backpacking through Europe because it would be cool to do Europe on a shoestring and was secretly hoping to find interesting men. Everything was fitting into place until I saw the sofa. A three-seater? What happened to the L-shaped one? No matter. I'd keep that to myself and give Toby and Alexis a call in the morning to make sure they were okay, that Lydia was okay, and to make sure that the slippage had passed without incident and was simply the result of too much aloneness. Too much loneliness.

LYDIA AND HER boyfriend signed a lease on a one-bedroom apartment with a small balcony; Toby called me to tell me.

"With Josh?" I asked.

"Who else?" he said. "It's a nice starter apartment. They found it themselves." His tone was neutral, as if he was stating a fact as inconsequential as a ten percent chance of rain. My son preferred facts, much the same way that he preferred his beef well cooked. He cringed at any trace of juice leaking from the solid structure of the meat. Medium-well was his limit. I hadn't had dinner with him and his family for a long time, but I doubt that he'd graduated to accepting a trace of pink, let alone drippings.

I hadn't seen Josh since he appeared at my door with

Lydia. To hear that he was still in the picture took me by surprise. I assumed that Lydia was too young and carefree to consider reining in a passion, taking on the grunt work of solid commitment, and hunkering down to test its shelf life. Where was the passion in that? "A two-bedroom?"

"No, no. A one-bedroom. A starter apartment, remember?" So she ended the pregnancy and didn't tell her father about the whole incident, I decided. "They're moving this weekend. We're giving her her bedroom furniture outright. Alexis will go through the kitchen to see if there's anything they can use that she doesn't really need. And then of course there are all the sheets and towels that we never use. Christ, some of them still have the price tags on them."

"Alexis will be taking care of that too, I suppose."

"Yep."

"And you?" I asked. "What are you taking care of?"

"I'm giving them a little mad money. Oh, and they're taking the living room sofa. The L-shaped one."

I didn't reply.

"You don't approve, do you," he said. "Fess up, Dad. The sofa is ugly. It's a fact. We'll get a new one. No big deal. Alexis is on board."

Ugliness doesn't count as a fact. Nevertheless, I kept this fact to myself and took a deep breath. The sofa deserved to stay in the family, ugly as it might be. Better that than ending up at a Goodwill store. "As you wish. Maybe they'll get around to reupholstering it one day. Make it less ugly. Tell me about Josh."

When Toby called with the news about the apartment, I couldn't tell whether he considered it to be a cause for celebration or tribulation. Either way, it wasn't the occasion to disclose a recent fact of my own to him: the refrigerator incident. I didn't want to alarm him and cause him to pounce on me with a litany of suggestions. We all have our versions of a refrigerator incident. Most of the time they cause a chuckle, especially when we're young. Like the time I almost wore my bedroom slippers to school until the driveway felt strange under my feet and I glanced down and saw two fuzzy Yogi Bear faces staring up at me. But sometimes they stop you in your tracks, especially when you're old, and make you wonder whether you're finally losing your grip.

A few weeks before Toby called, but after Lydia and her boyfriend had shown up at my front door, I opened the refrigerator door to take two eggs out for breakfast and found my underwear neatly folded and stacked on the shelf underneath the eggs, next to an assortment of cheeses that my doctor told me I should eliminate because of the competition between bad and good cholesterol levels. I removed the briefs and placed them in the underwear drawer in my bedroom. Everything else in the drawer was intact: T-shirts folded and layered to the right; socks rolled into neat balls and piled in the middle; multi-colored BVDs stuffed haphazardly to the left. The incident seemed harmless enough, almost funny.

Shoving the briefs into the drawer where they belonged, I remembered my father standing at the front door in front of my mother, Adrienne, and me and fuming over not being able to find his key ring, as if it were somehow our fault. Adrienne pointed out that the key ring was looped around his left index finger; the keys were hidden in his clenched fist. He was mortified, but the three of us were able to cajole him until he laughed and said, "Jesus! Let's go for some custard." These things happened, I told myself as I closed the underwear drawer. I tried to let the incident go, but no one was there to help me make light of it, to reassure me that placing my underwear in the refrigerator wasn't the telltale sign of some insidious condition that had found fertile ground in my brain where it would spawn and spread, causing incidents that could be harmful. The prospect terrified me. I made the rounds of the house to see if the oven and kitchen sink spigots were turned off, the front door locked, the windows closed. I was wasting my time. The danger lay in the endless possible oversights. My simple life in my modest home in Maple Grove Pointe suddenly seemed complex and treacherous. It was time to move to a setting that could protect me from my lapses. I didn't share this fact with Toby on the phone. It wouldn't have been fair to hijack his news of Lydia growing up with my news of diminishing. He did seem happy about her, which made me wonder whether he knew she was pregnant, or had been pregnant and was no longer.

"They're welcome to come by my place and take whatever they want," I told my son before we hung up the phone.

"That's okay, Dad. They'll have more than enough to get started," he said.

"I'll give them a call," I replied. "I could stand a purge." How curious I was to observe them, a young couple assessing my well-worn objects as possible accessories to their initiation into cohabitation. They could help themselves. Carte blanche. After I hung up the phone, I surveyed the objects I'd accumulated over the years. Each one had a story. Every story has an end.

THEY SHOWED UP on time. On the counter, I'd laid out a platter of imported cheeses and crackers that I was hoping they wouldn't be familiar with. They still had a lot to learn. Josh was not as tall as I'd remembered, or Lydia was taller than I'd remembered. "Take a gander," I told them. "I'll stay here in the kitchen."

"Grandpa, this is weird," she said. "It's your stuff."

"Try the cheese with the brown specks in it. Truffles. From Alba. Do you know where that is?"

"No."

"It's in Piedmont. Do you know where that is?"

She took a wedge. "This is all too weird."

"When were you against weird?" I asked her. "Not long

ago your hair was blue." I took her hand. "Take what you want. If it helps, imagine that I met a man who's super-rich and lives on the Main Line in a huge house that's completely furnished and he's asked me to move in with him and I love him and his house and everything in it."

She squeezed my hand. "That's amazing!" she said. "You've fallen in love again!"

I pulled back. "Sweetheart, at my age, falling can be deadly. Now go scavenge."

They went down the hall. Josh led the way. I heard her say, "He's losing it." Poking my head around the wall, I could see Josh pointing to a painting on the wall: four tanned and toned caballeros strutting along a beach in white button-down shirts, black jackets and slacks. Everything tapered except their wide-brimmed fedoras. "Virile, and with secrets" is how Len described the painting when he insisted on buying it. "We'll hang it in the living room. Stir things up a little." I agreed. Their shirts were unbuttoned below the sternum.

"That's kinda nice," Josh said. "What do you think?"

"Can't relate," I heard her say. "What does it have to do with anything that's us?"

I didn't hear him respond. Maybe he didn't respond, except by shrugging his shoulders the way he might do whenever they had a minor disagreement; or by unhooking the painting from the wall and carrying it under his arm as they proceeded down the hall because he really didn't care what she thought; or by making a fist at her and pointing it close to her face to remind her who was boss. How much did I know about my granddaughter and the boys she latched on to?

I took a piece of cheese and closed my eyes, waiting for the soft wedge to melt in my mouth and release the flavor of the truffles. In that circumscribed darkness, I decided that the painting was not up for grabs. I was in the habit of gawking at those men and making up stories about who they were and what they did together when no one was watching, especially when I focused on the small patch of dense chest hair on the second man from the right, who was my favorite. For me, that dark patch poking out of a white tapered shirt was the epicenter of the painting, the one that spawned all of my erotic fantasies about those four men, about all men, about me with men, occasionally about me with Len, even though he'd been dead for a while. Even without the stories I made up, those caballeros were excellent company. Happily stranded on the empty beach they were walking on, they made me feel less stranded in my tastefully furnished house. Lydia was right. The painting had nothing to do with who she was or what they might become together. Seated at the far end of my sofa, she was a study in suffering, but not from the trichophilia that had held her grandpa captive from the time that Donny removed his cap on a winter's day long, long ago.

I opened my eyes and contemplated taking a piece of cheese from the other side of the platter, a sickly yellow cheese with black specks in it. Poppy seeds? Or an unwanted growth like my mother's chin hairs. She tweezed her chin hairs on Wednesday evenings, the evening of the week when Len and I paid my parents a visit. After dinner, she had no qualms about going to the den, turning on the television, kicking back in her black leatherette chair and plucking away. She kept a pair of tweezers and a hand mirror with 10X magnification on the end table near her chair, beside the glass ashtray that she emptied after stubbing out a second or third butt but never got around to washing. The ashtray had a perpetual gray film on it. Her lower jaw protruded like a bulldog's as she angled the tweezers toward each follicle on her chin that sprouted the advancing enemy.

"Look at her," Len said. "How adorable."

"I'm glad you think so," I replied. "I think it's disgusting."

"One more thing to not like about your mother. Let's see what adorable rituals you take on when you're her age. I hope I don't find them disgusting."

We sat on the sofa and watched television with them, my father quickly dozing off, my mother plucking away. "Len," I said, "You have my permission to kill me on the spot if you ever see me doing anything like that in a public place." But he died before he could see me shaving my ears. The large mirror in our master bathroom was framed by small round lightbulbs, whose total wattage could have lit the entire house; concentrated around a mirror, the blazing light brought into relief the pores and creases on my face, and the bramble of hair that was everywhere on each ear: the lobe, the helix and antihelix, the fossa, the concha. Why hadn't anyone had the kindness or the balls to tell me? Not Len. He would have attacked those hairs with a passion. I could imagine him sneaking up behind me in the bathroom and pulling a few of them out with his teeth before working his mouth down the nape of my neck to heat me up. Yes, both of us loved sex—the animal kind and the love-making kind. As the years of getting into bed together every night went by and the familiarity of each other in bed together every night dulled our erotic desires for each other, the tip of Len's index finger found its way to some part of my body as we settled into sleep, even when I was turned away from him on my side of the bed—the right side, which had been established from the get-go. That bit of finger was his envoy. "I'm here," it said. I wished that for Toby and Alexis; and now, standing in the kitchen, I wished it for Lydia and what's-his-name too. So much boiled down to that.

Once a week, I shaved my ears with a plastic disposable razor until I couldn't see any more hairs, although when I ran my finger along the flesh protecting the curve of cartilage I could still feel stubble. Afterward, I sometimes stretched my arms behind me and let my fingers roam around my upper shoulders to survey what had taken root there. A few stray hairs, as far as I could feel, and a vague sense of fuzz. At that moment, the utility of a 10X hand mirror became clear. "Where did my mother's hand mirror end up?" I wondered.

A few days later, I bought the cheapest 10X hand mirror I could find at the nearby Walmart, which is always nearby, and shoved it to the back of the bottom drawer beside the bathroom sink. My little secret. The mirror was too large and the drawer didn't shut completely. I put it on the counter—next to the tri-color stoneware soap dispenser that Len and I had purchased on a side street in Coimbra—for all the world to see. All the world. All my world. How many guests would I have, and of those, how many would need to use my bathroom? And of those, how many would notice a hand mirror on the counter and wonder what that was all about as they wiped their ass, washed their hands or flushed the toilet?

I heard their footsteps.

"You're still in the kitchen?" Lydia asked.

"Yep. The cheese is really delicious. Have the last wedge of the truffled one."

"Josh, you take it."

Right. His name was Josh. He took the wedge and popped it into his mouth like it was a Cheeto. "Mmm," he said. "Good."

"Grandpa, there's a lot of stuff here that we could use but..."

"Consider it yours. I'll be moving soon. The place is smaller."

"I thought the guy was rich."

"What rich guy?"

"The one you said you were moving in with on the Main Line."

"Oh right. That one. I called him while you were looking around and told him we were done." I raised an eyebrow. "Sweet gullible thing. Did you really believe that?"

"So you're not in love?"

"At my age?"

"Why not?"

"Why?"

Josh clasped her upper arm. "Honey, we need to get going."

I liked the word "honey" coming from his chapped full lips. It sounded perfectly natural, as if it had been bestowed upon him as a reward for a long-settled partnership, so unlike the way he used "sir" to me when we'd first laid eyes on each other.

"Go," I said. "You make the arrangements to pick up the stuff that you want. Leave me a couple of rolls of toilet paper if you don't mind."

As they headed toward the front door, she stopped, turned around and squeezed me tight. "Grandpa, you're the best."

The best at what? Being foolish? Generous? Understanding? A clueless old man? "Leave me the painting in the hall too."

They rented a U-Haul trailer to haul off their bounty. I kept a low profile in the front yard as they went back and forth from house to trailer like worker bees serving their higher purpose. Only once did I speak. Lydia was struggling with a small but cumbersome cedar trunk. I was worried about her overdoing it. Josh was trailing behind with an armful of linens.

"Let me take those," I said to him as I held out my arms. "Go help Lydia. You know, what with the baby and all."

He looked at me. "She's not pregnant."

I lowered my arms. "She's not?"

He continued toward the trailer. "Not anymore."

Lydia lifted the trailer ramp and pushed it back into its slot while Josh started the car. He picked up speed when the car and trailer had cleared the driveway and were on the street. Lydia stuck her hand outside the passenger window and waved. I didn't wave back, too taken up by wondering whether she had terminated the pregnancy or whether the pregnancy had been taken away from her of its own accord. She and Josh seemed solid enough. I guess it didn't matter.

First stop, the hall. The painting was still there. I stood in front of those four men, staring at them without blinking until my eyes burned and teared and made the scene inside the frame go liquid enough to convince myself that one of the men was smiling at me. I could almost hear him say, "Gracias, amigo." My body flushed with heat. "Thank God you're all still here," I blurted. I proceeded to the bedroom, on the prowl for the empty spaces that moments ago had been furnished with the props of my life. Some absences were blatant, like Len's Bentwood chair that I'd repurposed as a repository for odds and ends of clothing that needed to be inspected before hanging them up or tossing them into the hamper. Those large absences gave air and relief. The smaller absences were more troublesome, like the baseball card of Sandy Koufax that was no longer leaning against the night lamp on my side of the bed. A gift from Len with his inscription: "Koufax is sexier, but you won't strike out with me." He'd given it to me during a ball game while I was eating a hot dog. The corner of the card had a mustard stain on it. I aborted my mission of inspecting the other rooms. It was already clear to me that the trivial could stand out, the conspicuous be forgotten altogether, and that my curated version of my history was random and chaotic.

Next and last stop, the kitchen, where the terry cloth dish towel lay balled up on the counter. I gazed out the window above the sink, my favorite window. The night sky was clear, moonless, flickering with a billion stars when I stared hard enough and didn't blink. If only I could spread my aged and brittle wings and soar into the endless expanse of starry details laid bare by the absence of moonlight, but the dish towel needed to be smoothed along the oven door in order to dry completely by morning; otherwise it would have that dank smell and need to be washed, even though I'd taken it from the towel drawer only the day before. Besides, I was exhausted from the day. I longed to kick back in bed and read a passage or two from a choice classic before dozing off, a paragraph containing long sentences with purposeful digressions neatly set off with paired punctuation marks, lots of them—capricious commas and parentheses and dashes jockeying for a prominent position before the meandering sentence came up against the full stop. But I was too tired to rummage for such a book among the shelves and table tops. I adjusted the dish towel and went to my bed, which was still there. Lydia and Josh hadn't taken it, thank goodness. The mattress was king size, too big for them. They were young and still needed an abundance of intertwining if they were ever to be able to safely navigate the perils of detachment from time to time and still find safe harbor. I sank into the middle of the mattress and stretched my arms like a crucifix. My hands didn't reach the edges of the bed. Yes, it was big. Almost big enough for me to live on.

LYDIA AND JOSH called it quits a week before they were planning to announce their engagement. Josh kept the apartment and Lydia moved back home. Toby called me and told me the news, but not before he'd asked me how I was and I said fine.

"She's a mess," he said.

"Who wouldn't be?"

"She shouldn't be," he said, with growing exasperation. "She's the one who left him. At least from the way she tells it."

It made sense to me. The resolute one is the one to crash when resoluteness is no longer required and the churning sets in. "How is Josh holding up?"

"Who cares?" he said.

I cared. Truth was, I was pleased for the two of them. My truth insisted that first attempts at domesticating love are supposed to fail. Love takes practice, like solitude and every other tough act that calls for building muscle while staying limber. What's to be gained if you're convinced you got it right the first time? "Give her a peck on the cheek for me, poor thing."

"I will."

"And do me a favor."

"What's that?"

"Don't hate him. That's too easy. You're smart enough not to go that route."

"I'll think on it."

I waited for him to continue. Apparently that was all he had to say. "Another thing," I said. "If and when they divvy up their possessions, I don't want any of my stuff back."

"But it's yours," he reminded me.

"It won't fit in the new place."

"Dad, what the hell are you talking about?"

"The move."

"What move?"

"I'm moving, son. To an apartment. A smaller one. I'm graduating. To less."

He waited for me to continue, but I had nothing more to say at the moment, so we hung up the phone after one of us inevitably said he needed to get off and the other said okay.

Three

Alexis called me on the morning of the move and offered to bring dinner to the new place. Toby shouted in the background, "We can come a few hours early to help you set up house."

"Don't worry," she said. "We won't interfere. Think of us as quiet worker bees waiting for you to tell us what to put where."

I was about to say, "That's okay," to fend them off but I couldn't bring myself to. They might be offended and resist offering to help again. One day, I would probably need it. I dropped the "that's" and simply said, "Okay."

When they arrived, the aluminum tray of lasagne Alexis was cradling in her arms made the usual hug impossible. I could feel the warmth of the tray near my belly as she bent over to kiss my cheek, after which I brought my index finger to the spot she kissed to locate the grease of a lipstick mark. Toby was by her side, embracing a wooden bowl of salad the size of a satellite dish, and didn't try to hug me even though he was a bear-hugger. Always had been. Lydia was behind them, almost hidden by the front line of her parents. I wasn't expecting her at all. A canvas bag was slung over her right shoulder. Probably wine or some dessert concoction that her parents made her carry in order to give specificity to their collective thoughtfulness. "You're part of this family too," I could hear them say. Her hair was pulled back in a tight bun and she'd applied soft touches of make-up that were meant to go under the radar of most men, but not mine. Her eyebrows were straighter than I remembered them being and her clipped fingernails were unpainted. Chaste. Or chastened. Who'd put her up to this rendition of growing up?

"Cute place," she said as she walked through the front door. Cute? Puppies were cute. Twelve-year-olds holding hands could be cute. Old men making stupid decisions could be construed as cute, I supposed. I studied her face to see what she might mean. Nothing.

"Thank you, sweetie," I said.

"Where should I put this?" she asked. "It's dessert."

"Wonderful. What is it?"

"I don't know," she said. "Mom got it at the supermarket on the way over here."

"You can put it on the kitchen counter." I pointed a finger toward the small alcove kitchen. The gesture was superfluous since the kitchen was a few feet away.

Alexis followed her with the lasagne. "This'll need to be reheated a bit," she said. "Do you have an oven?"

"If you scan the kitchen counter at eye level, you'll see a microwave. Below it is a four-burner stove. Below that is an oven. It's complicated, I know."

She made her way to the kitchen area, whose path was obstructed by a rolled-up area rug. The bulk of the lasagne tray might prevent her from seeing the rug as she approached it. I said nothing.

Without asking, Toby set the salad bowl on the small bistro table in the living area; the bowl would need to be moved somewhere else once we sat down to eat at the table, which was the only table that could accommodate four. In my other house, and the house before that, the bistro table was the "you never know" table that ended up in an empty corner of an unused room, where it served as a waystation for objects whose final destination hadn't been determined: supermarket flyers and envelopes marked "Resident" that might be of interest one day; knickknacks purchased in tourist shops during vacations that might retain their charm in their new location one day. "Bistro" indeed. "Repository for domestic landfill" was more apt. In my new compact home, it was restored to its intended function. Gone was the dining room table that had two leaves, eight chairs and a matching credenza. The set was picked up by a lovely young couple who told me it was exactly what they were looking for. "We love teak," the husband said, clasping his wife by her waist and pulling her closer to him as he said it. They were sweet and enthusiastic. "The price is flexible," I told them. They proposed twenty percent less than what was written on the tag during my yard sale. "Very flexible," I said. I'd have given it to them for free, but they didn't go that far.

"Let's get going," Toby said. "Where should we start?"

I surveyed the room to take in the artifacts of my history. Spartan. Was this all I had to show for myself?

"Why don't we eat," I said. "I can take care of everything on my own. The movers did a terrific job."

"We came to help," Alexis said.

Their solicitousness was grating on me. "I appreciate that, but I've got plenty of time. It'll give me something to do."

We sat around the small table, occasionally brushing feet as we figured out a way to fit comfortably into such a small space. We ate large portions of lasagne, which was delicious. Each portion that Alexis pried loose with the spatula was a perfect square and remained intact as it traveled from tray to plate. I expected nothing less of her, but I was nevertheless impressed and gorged myself on the swell of family.

"Remember how I used to cry when I was little if we had to wait to be seated at a restaurant?" Toby said. "And you'd go and pinch some breadsticks from a waiter to tide me over?"

"And how I had to cut your meat for you until you were ten because you were afraid of holding a knife?" I added.

The swell of family didn't last long. Lydia brought the canvas bag to the table and removed a transparent plastic container of pre-packaged fruit salad sealed with an adhesive strip displaying the price and bar-code label, followed by four Styrofoam dessert bowls and four plastic forks. I expected Alexis to take over, but it was Lydia who snapped open the lid and began dishing the fruit into the bowls. Alexis was fixed on Toby, who finally nodded his head.

"By the way, Dad," he said. "We're going to be moving too." Lydia handed him a bowl of fruit salad. He passed it to me. "All of us. Not together, though. In fact, none of us together."

Alexis chimed in. "Actually, we're skipping that stage," she said. "We're getting divorced. No drama, though. We're good." She reached for my son's hand, which he duly gave her.

I studied the fruit salad. I'd need to pick out most of the melon chunks, which were too ripe and mushy at the top, too hard and green at the bottom. "What about you, Lydia?"

"She was accepted at Georgetown University, in D.C.," Alexis said. "Or is it George Washington University? Oh dear." She paused. "Anyway, both good schools. In D.C."

Toby added, "I'm moving to Madison. I accepted a job there."

I looked at Alexis. "That leaves you."

"I'm going to Fort Collins. In Colorado."

"I know where Fort Collins is."

"I'll be staying with my sister and brother-in-law until I figure out what I want to do. You remember them, don't you?"

"If you mean Sheryl with the not-so-great nose job and Gerry who always buttons the top button of his button-down shirts, yes, I remember them. I remember their two kids too. Rebecca and Casey. She's the smart one, he's athletic. Isn't that how you describe them?"

I looked at Lydia again. "D.C.?"

Alexis intervened again. "She was considering going to..."

I interrupted her. "I was asking Lydia. Let her talk, for Chrissake. She's an adult. Remember?"

"I'm sorry. You're right. It's just that I..."

I interrupted her again. "Alexis. Help yourself to some fruit salad."

My question to Lydia got lost in the scooping of fruit and passing of bowls, the swift downing of hothouse melon and flavorless berries. Lydia was first to empty her bowl. "Dad, I'm super tired," she said.

My bowl was half full. "Me too," I said, rising from my seat. "Leave everything. I can clean up."

Alexis rose, gathered the bowls and forks and took them to the kitchen. When she returned, I said, "That's enough."

As they made their way down the darkness of the driveway to the car, I almost shouted, "Please, don't go!" so they'd turn toward me and I'd shepherd them back into the house where we'd redo the evening, and when they re-left I'd be able to feel what I usually felt when we spent an evening together: My family, and me at the core of it all. I watched them fading into the night. When had I lost my magic touch to hold us together, to matter to them? Or was it Len who had the magic touch?

Lydia sprinted back to me and gave me a hug. My hand cupped the back of her head and fiddled with her bun until her hair fell down her back. So thick and healthy. She whispered in my ear, "I'll call you tomorrow."

"Whenever you want."

She didn't call the next day. No one called the next day. A few days went by before my phone rang—an automatic message about my upcoming appointment with Dr. Lapinsky, my neurologist. "Press 1 to confirm." You'd think his receptionist could have made the call for the sake of the human touch, the notion of bedside manner, even if she was annoying. Brittany, I think her name was. Whenever I came to the office, saw her behind the open plexiglass window of the reception counter and said, "Hello there! How are you?" she took my question seriously as she handed me the clipboard with the forms I needed to complete each time I arrived.

What could I write down that they didn't already read? She'd start by saying how well her children were doing and would quickly segue into their difficulties. Difficulties that she felt responsible for because of her own difficulties, she'd add. "Well, I'd better start filling out these forms," I'd say, turning away from her and the drama of her particular unhappiness that she seemed intent on finding an audience for. Same ritual every time. The forms were always the same too: requests to provide my medical history for the nth time. I was tempted to introduce some new and outrageous condition in the "Additional information" box—an iron lung, pacemaker or catheter newly embedded under my softening flesh—to see if Dr. Lapinsky or any of his staff would notice and make a remark. Regardless, I was grateful for the automated call. I'd forgotten about the appointment entirely.

THE MORNING AFTER the failed tasty lasagne and family fission, I propped up the pillows behind my head and lingered in bed, the very bed that Len and I bought when we moved in together a billion years ago; same white 1500 thread-count sheets that were our favorites regardless of the season, and the navy-blue down blanket we'd ease out of the cedar chest every winter. The bed, the blanket, the sheets and pillows. Soft sanctuary against the hard edges of last night. Too many family members to make adjusted versions of. And then all the remaining boxes to unpack and decide where, in these unlived-in rooms, their contents can provide the hope that a sense of continuity, of meaning, might stand a chance of pressing on. The brick and mortar of my life stacked in boxes or dispersing to faraway cities; everything to be deconstructed and reassembled in a new way. Too much seismic activity for someone my age. Best to stay in bed and play around with fleshing out the firefly dream that had been interrupted by my need to pee and that didn't resume after I found my way to the new bathroom, emptied my bladder and burrowed back under the blanket. As a child, I could will a dream to pick up where it left off if an incursion of wakefulness had tried to abort it. "Chapter sleeping," I called it when I explained it to my father. He wasn't impressed. "You read too much," he said. He preferred a son who was more athletic. The chapter sleeping stopped when I started having nocturnal emissions. I didn't tell him about my rite of passage, impressed as he might have been, because he'd probably have said something to not let on that he was.

The only window in my bedroom has an eastern exposure, which is disorienting, what with all the light of the waking sun arriving much earlier than what I'm used to in the morning. How can I possibly languish in a dreamscape with such a gathering force of brightness? I should have chosen a unit with a western exposure.

I lowered my eyelids and all faded to an almost darkness, the color of my son's first car, a used Oldsmobile Cutlass Supreme. Pewter.

"It's clunky," he said when I pointed it out in the lot.

"Solid though," I replied. "The price is reasonable, and I can talk the sales rep down a little." Toby didn't react. "Nice color, too. Don't you think?" I added.

"What's so nice about gray?"

"Not gray. Pewter. Elegant. Definitely a boy color."

This morning, as I lingered in bed, the pewter produced by my closed lids shielded enough light for the fireflies of the dream to make themselves seen. A profusion of them at eye level flickering above a yard. My childhood yard, I can tell, by the smell of the dream—bird-pecked crab apples and plums fallen to the ground and emitting the reek of their slow rot into the zoysia grass that my father had meticulously seeded with his tow-behind broadcast spreader. I can tell by the texture of the dream—the sponginess of the zoysia under my bare feet, and the soft grazing of the weeping willow branches that my hair gets tangled in as I weave in and out trying to catch the fireflies in my cupped hands. I can tell by a visual—a second set of hands, the hands that are freckled above the knuckles, topped by long and graceful fingernails caked with grime under their edges—clutching a mason jar. The hands I've always wanted to clasp—Donny's hands—but which, in this moment of the dream, are otherwise engaged by a mason jar as he darts about trying to capture enough of these pinpricks of light to transform the jar into a lantern. He stops suddenly and turns toward me. "Hey, Reds!" he calls out. "Stick out your hand."

"What for?" I ask.

"Shut up and trust me," he says.

When I oblige him (and I must oblige him in whatever he asks of me because that's what I think love is), he sets the mason jar on the grass. With the thumb and index finger of his left hand he takes hold of my ring finger; with the other thumb and index finger he squishes a firefly and smears its phosphorescent paste around the base of my extended finger until it forms a slender band, like a wedding ring. "There," he says. I look into his eyes, which are already looking into mine. Before he can ask me the question that I'm sure he's about to ask, I say, "I do."

He smiles. "Which of our last names should we use?"

"Armstrong."

"Why mine?" he asks, bending toward me, pleased.

Before I can answer him, and before he might have kissed me, my eyes opened, as they must have done last night when, as he was bending toward me in the dream itself, I woke up because I had to pee.

The sunlight was strong and caused the fireflies to fade,

together with whatever other particles of the dream might have revealed enough of themselves to help me cobble the whole story. The slow-to-accrete heat was allied with the light, penetrating the single-pane window and pulling me away from the dream haze and toward the harsher, more brutal edges of the boxes stacked along the windowed wall. Their sides were clearly labeled in thick blue magic marker: "Sweaters," "Shoes," "Socks & undies," "Bthrm linens." The categories were of no use to me. I couldn't recall a single sweater, sneaker, sock or washcloth that the boxes contained. The highest of them was perched on the stack that rose above the windowsill, shielding a chunk of heat and light from entering the room. "Len misc," the label read. How was this possible? There was nothing miscellaneous about Len, and just like that the dreamscape disintegrated entirely. I was back in the clutches of the day, its boxes to unpack, a new home to set up, a history to propel forward, even if I didn't know where I was. Toby, Alexis, Lydia. They were the ones who'd left. I was the one who was unmoored.

WHEN TOBY CALLED the first time after the lasagne in my new house, I didn't know who it was until he said "Dad" a few sentences in and started describing his new house. Outside my living room window, the rhododendrons edging my lawn were beginning to bloom. Spring. Alexis had brought her lasagne when it was snowing outside. An appropriate winter meal. That much time had passed since we'd last spoken. No wonder I didn't recognize his voice.

"Four bedrooms, three baths on half an acre," he gloated. "And a fully finished basement." Was he planning to marry again, breed again and put all those bedrooms to good use? Only days before, I'd had a flicker of a marriage fantasy of my own. The spouse-to-be was the neighbor above me whose zealous use of gym equipment each night made me have to ramp up the volume of my television to forty-two. I ran into him by the dumpsters in the parking lot. He introduced himself. "Harvey," he said. "I think I live above you." I was about to say, "Believe me, I know," but he added, "You must be a great cook. The smells that come into my living room are fantastic," and I saw him beyond the grating factor of the ruckus he made each night. He was an extremely fit version of a man in his early seventies: taut flesh, smooth and neatly clipped fingernails, upper lip not wearied into a razor-thin line, full head of wavy silver hair. In short, sexy. Still, who needs it? For all I knew, the daily meds and supplements he took made his flesh smell metallic; he could also wear Depends. And then there was the division of labor to negotiate if we were to share a home. He probably had a wife anyway. And if he didn't, there must have been a compelling reason. No, he wasn't someone to get entangled with.

"The house sounds nice," I said to my son.

"You should visit sometime. There's plenty of room."

"I'd say so. Four bedrooms and three baths. All on the upper floors? Lots of steps." I asked how Lydia was.

"Fine," he said and leapt into enumerating her accomplishments at school, finishing with, "She already has a boyfriend. Pre-med."

"So Jewish of you. Why is this pre-med different from all other pre-meds?"

"Dad."

"I'm joking, son. What color is Lydia's hair these days?"

I could hear him laughing. "You should call her sometime."

Visit him. Call her. His directives annoyed me. Why should I be the one to make an effort? I was responsible for their existence. And now I was old. The Elder. "How's Alexis?"

"We haven't spoken. I imagine she's fine. Remember, she was the one who initiated the divorce."

I didn't remember, but I trusted him. "She must have been convinced there was a better path for her."

He paused as if he were digesting bitter fruit. "We'll come

around to being friends one day."

Sweet. I waited for him to ask me how I was, but he didn't. I forgave him. There are only so many states of mental agitation and physical decline that one can shoulder. No need to add mine to his own. Fathers are meant to be immutable bedrocks, even if they are shrinking from osteoporosis, snagged by memory lapses, reluctant to venture beyond the two-mile radius that is adventure enough. If he'd asked me how I was, I'd have said, "Fine."

"It was good to hear from you, Tobeleh. Congratulations on the new home."

"Thanks, Dad. We'll talk soon?"

"Sure," I said. I hung up before he might have muttered, "Love you." The alarm on my phone was blipping. Time to take my statins. I also needed to pee, which was more urgent than the statins. Standing in front of the toilet bowl, I was overcome by such sadness about how foolish we can be to believe that everything will work out precisely as we'd imagined that I forgot to raise the lid. What a mess I made.

THE RHODODENDRONS HAVE shed most of their flowers onto the common ground. There they lie for long stretches, since the lawns get mowed less frequently in autumn. I still haven't visited my son or my granddaughter. Each season offers a rationale for me to stay put: too hot, too cold, too variable. I look forward to Toby's phone calls every Sunday around breakfast, although I wish he'd be less programmatic about it. It reduces me to an item that's been slotted into his to-do list, a chore to be gotten over with so he can move on to the more interesting and value-added items. During the phone calls, I expect to hear Alexis scuffling in the background until she realizes it's me he's talking to, after which she'll advance to the foreground, bend toward the phone, and say a few well-meaning words before she ends with, "I'll leave you two men alone. Now don't say bad things about me!" Then I remember that she's nowhere near Toby's house; that he lives alone in a large house in Madison, and she lives in a faraway state. For the life of me, I can't remember which one.

He updates me on the events of his week—the broken washing machine that eludes his attempts to repair it, the cracked clay on the tennis court that he's reported to the HOA for the second time, the plantation shutters he installed in one of the extra bedrooms after a three-week delay in delivery. His events occasionally extend to his workplace, but the business lexicon he enters into prevents me from understanding what it is he actually does to earn the six-figure income he reminds me about too often. All of his anecdotes are devoid of people's names. He prefers categories—a neighbor of his, a colleague of his, a friend of his. He's insistent about this.

"Does your friend have a name?" I asked him once.

"Of course he does," he replied without then telling me what it was. Curious. Does he not want to confuse me with a flurry of names that he assumes will go in one ear and out the other? Or is this nameless person not yet a friend and may never be one because he doesn't have friends; he only has people who have the potential to be useful to him? So little do I understand about the adult version of my son, especially since he divorced and moved away, which I can't hold against him. It wasn't intentional. Just one of the hidden trip wires of midlife and the bout of drift that follows.

To his credit, he's learned to ask me how I am. I say, "Fine," waiting for him to inquire further, which he doesn't.

"That's great." Eventually, he says, "Dad, you really should visit sometime." He's able to make it sound sincere, since he knows that I won't come. It also signals his desire to bring the phone call to an end.

Whatever he has to say to me, I listen attentively. It's my only ingress into the people and props of his daily life, unless I can find it in me to hop on a plane, go to him, and settle into one of his spare rooms for a few days. In reality, I'm soaking up the sound of his voice more than listening to what it has to say. The elixir of it.

Lydia calls me rarely and at such strange hours (midnight, five in the morning) that something must be up. I slap my cheeks to bring me to instant wakefulness. Like her father, she begins with a list—the great friends she's making, the great grades she's getting, the great times she's having. I'm no longer a believer in greatness, especially when insisted upon first thing and at ungodly hours. Yes, something must be up. She's hurting somewhere deep down and is baiting me, the Elder, to locate and excise it. Abracadabra. She used to be all outpourings of highs and lows, her hugs cloying and long. Unabashed. Delicious. The smell of her hair pushing against my face and tickling my nose. She's older now.

When she comes to understand by my reticence that I'm not going to come through in the way I believe she wishes me to, she finds a reason to end the call: her cat is meowing to be fed; she has to check that she locked the front door; she should get back to studying. "We'll talk again soon," she says.

I'd like to tell her to call at a more civilized hour, but what hour might that be? Eleven o'clock in the morning? Four o'clock in the afternoon? A strong dose of weariness accompanies any hour of my day.

"Call any time, Matchstick."

My son. My granddaughter. I mind that both of them have moved away. Terribly. The commotion of their chatter when they arrive, the energy of their movements during their visits, the falling back into exquisite calm when they finally go home. A riptide of swelling, crashing, receding safely protected within a large, intimate love. Then they pack up their belongings and set up life elsewhere, my bulwark against stasis, against blundering too far. I try resenting them—How dare they pull out and away! How selfish of them!—but I can't blame them for being eager to push on, wings nimble, vision keen, talons on the ready to snatch at anything that might satisfy their hunger. It's not their fault that my appetite is hardly what it used to be, that my days are leaden.

THE FIRST SNOWS arrive at the end of October, light dustings of flakes that melt as soon as they contact the still-warm earth. It takes about a month before any snow begins to stick. How lovely to raise the shades on such a morning and find the light more blinding than that of a midsummer afternoon and all activity come to a halt. I imagine everyone hunkered down in their homes and I don't feel so alone. Often, when a snow-covered day comes to a close, I realize that I haven't thought about my family at all, let alone missed them. No guilt. Only relief, as if I've achieved some major stride, although I can't figure out what it is. There are other in-my-marrow people who go off my radar for even longer, regardless of the season. Those whose absence goes further back. Len, for example. And Donny. And then there are the more recent ones—Eugene and Harvey, whom I don't think about at all, although they make visitations as I'm getting ready for bed, night-blooming cereuses in my arid landscape. I grab the two pillows on the right side of the bed, the side that Len slept on, and tuck one of them between my legs; the other I scrunch up against my chest and wrap my arms around. I curl into a fetal position and fall asleep quickly. Deeply. So deeply sometimes that when I wake up in the morning, I'm in the same position and curse myself. "Damn," I say inside. "Bone against bone all night? My joints are going to be acting up all day."

The most recent person in my life is Mrs. Ramsey. Like Harvey, she is a neighbor, though not attached to my unit by a wall or ceiling. We encountered each other on the sidewalk one morning. She was ahead of me. Her glistening auburn hair finished in a perfectly straight line across the middle of her back. Her skirt was well above the knee, despite the cold.

Her hot pink socks were the same color as her thick hairband. When she paused to rummage through her tiny shoulder bag, I overtook her and managed to see her face. She was at least my age, poor thing. Still, I was cordial. "Good morning," I said. "How are you?" She stood in the middle of the sidewalk and recounted her life story, grasping my upper arm from time to time, inching closer toward me like some beast of prey. I was petrified.

"What about you?" she asked.

I didn't tell her my life story, but I made sure to refer to my late husband before saying, "I should get going. Nice to meet you." I accelerated my pace and didn't look back.

Mrs. Ramsey stopped by a few days later with some freshly baked corn muffins. I thanked her at the door but didn't let her in.

"I'll bring your plate back tomorrow," I said. "That was so kind of you."

"You can toss it. It's only one of those fancy aluminum trays." The muffins had canned corn niblets in them. A few days later, she followed up with her homemade biscuits stuffed with grape jelly. Without a doubt, she was creative. Also nosy. On both occasions, I could see her eyes scrutinizing everything that was visible beyond the slender band of my slightly opened front door.

"They smell delicious," I said. "I might have to ask you for the recipe."

She dropped by later with the recipe handwritten on a three-by-five card. I thanked her again and didn't let her in again. The recipe had many steps and called for ingredients in amounts that were too precise for me: three-eighths of this, two-fifths of that. I tossed the card in the kitchen bin and made sure to bury it beneath the banana peel and melon rind in case Mrs. Ramsey should manage to insinuate herself into my house and start rummaging through my garbage. I wouldn't put it past her. I'm not fond of Mrs. Ramsey. I won't let her in my house. She means well but the tentacles of her loneliness are more than I can handle.

By and large all the neighbors are friendly. Some of them have dogs. The dogs seem friendly enough too, but when the larger ones approach, I tighten up. Will they be content to sniff me from the knees down, or are they priming themselves for a more aggressive inspection? Something that might draw blood?

By the time I finish breakfast in winter, the sunlight is almost as strong as it's going to be for the day and I'm convinced that I know far less than other people believe themselves to know. This fact, if it's a true one, doesn't bother me. It would be nice to find other people who've arrived at the same conclusion, although I do wonder what we'd do together that would be all that different from being with people who haven't reached this conclusion. We'd certainly talk less. Ask fewer questions, offer fewer answers. This could be a welcome thing. Or it could make the condition of loneliness an even steeper descent.

WE TRAVELED A lot, Len and I. He was in charge of suitcase selection—small enough to manage easily, but not so small that we risked having their zippers split as we strained to close them. We went to Europe six times and visited forty-three U.S. states on road trips before he died. No organized tours, he insisted, even though he made a beeline for the touristic sites as soon as we settled into our lodgings.

"Is that all you're interested in?" I asked him in Paris after we power-walked from the Eiffel Tower to the Arc de Triomphe and down the Champs-Elysees to the Louvre without stopping to grab a crepe from a food truck, sit on a bench, pull at the warm dough, and eat and watch.

"I prefer going backward," he said. "Get them out of the way. Then we can amble. Fall into situations. Breathe them."

Never did an item inside our suitcases go unused; not once did either of us say, "We should have brought..." or "Why did we bring..." Len was a master at assessing the whole of a desire and then extrapolating essentials of need and economies of space. It never occurred to me to thank him for this. He wasn't doing it for me. He was doing it because that's what he did. It was Len being Len in the only way he could be.

Living with Len-being-Len for so many years must have altered me-being-me. This apartment, for example. Much smaller than what I ever imagined I could live in, even under the one scenario that defied imagining: living alone. Yet I chose it from among other larger options whose higher price tags were within my budget. Wherever I position myself, I can see all of its vaguely articulated spaces. No risk of getting lost. There are multiple windows on most walls, and all of the windows have screens. I take in light, I breathe in fresh air. If I can absorb these root elements with intention, I'll loom larger than my diminished self. Simple solutions to existential conundrums. So Len of me. I should have thanked him.

I still drive, take my walks. Both give me pleasure, although they require more effort and concentration than they used to, which maintains my flight patterns at low altitudes. This is something of a loss. Who doesn't want to feel from time to time that they are flying outside the contours of their life? That impulsive acts and feeling things intensively as if for the first time are still possible? And the low altitudes aren't without their risks either. Who wants to bang into a tree, trip over a crack on the sidewalk, or fall off a stepladder? Especially at my age. The potential calamity of the broken hip and its aftermath lurks everywhere.

As small as my apartment is, it would have been nice to have the L-shaped sofa find a place. A coming-full-circle kind of thing, even if full circles exist only in geometry, along with the tidy formulae for radii, diameters and circumferences that Miss Pugh scribbled with a fury on the blackboard in eighth-grade geometry. She pressed the chalk so hard that crumbs of it broke off and fell into the eraser tray, and when she tried to erase the blackboard, traces of the formulae remained, like precious Truths. She had a sense of humor about the subject of geometry, though, which made it stick and seem plausible and possibly relevant. That's why I've retained a lot of geometry, and Miss Pugh. Humor is important. Otherwise there's a blandness about most things, and a gentle creep of sadness—about what could have been, what should have been. What is. And dread about what is yet to come. If only I could pick Miss Pugh's brain about full circles, now that I've had decades of life to scope them out. She must be long dead. Her hair was blue-rinsed and reeked of Aqua Net hairspray even way back then.

"HAPPY BIRTHDAY, DAD!"

I glanced at the digital clock on my night table. Large blue numbers. Seven-seventeen a.m. Cool breeze funneling through the slit of open window and reminding me that it's spring. April. My birthday. The big seven-0. So early for him to call. Was he hoping to be the first? Did he want to get it out of the way so that he could get on with his day? Was he being solicitous to someone he perceived as an old man growing feeble and ineffectual? Or was the early call propelled by an impulse less fraught and entirely unexpected: the love of a son for his dad?

"Thanks, Tobeleh."

"What's special on your agenda for today?"

Agenda? Did he really use that word? With me? Ick. "Nothing really. But it's still early."

"Did I wake you up?" He sounded disappointed.

"Too late."

He told me that my gift was waiting in my inbox. "A boarding pass," he said. "You're coming to visit me. Us, to be precise. Lydia'll be here too. She's arriving later today. You tomorrow."

"Toby, I..."

"Non-refundable flight. Economy Plus. A car will pick you up at your house at ten tomorrow morning and take you to the airport. I'll meet you at baggage claim on the other end. Try to bring carry-on if you can. It's only four days. You don't need much."

"Toby, I..."

"Gotta run. Happy birthday. See you tomorrow!" He added, "Love you," before hanging up. Son of a bitch.

Rays of sunlight poured in between the slats of the blinds to illuminate a blizzard of dust motes in the air. My bedroom was transformed into an unsettling pointillist painting. This is what we breathe in day in day out? A galaxy of tiny solid particles? A miracle that we can live to be seventy.

I eased Len's go-to suitcase off the top shelf in the hallway linen closet: a compact army-green two-wheeler with dozens of airline tags looped around its extendable handle. Len had refused to yank them off despite my objections. "Leave them there," he'd say. "They don't get in the way and they'll remind us of times that'll make us smile." Before putting the suitcase away, he'd toss a few mothballs inside, which made it smell like camphor always. A protective smell. Curative, like the Vicks my mother put in the canister of the vaporizer on nights when my nose was stuffed and my body achy. As soon as the oversized contraption started to gurgle, she'd say to me, "Now breathe this in and you'll feel better," and then walk out of my bedroom, leaving me alone with this scary dark green monster ejecting steam from its stainless-steel proboscis.

Donny's backpack smelled of day-old ground meat and orange-flavored gumdrops and was mottled like the camouflage gear of a soldier slinking through enemy territory. His backpack, which he carried everywhere, was always filled to bursting, even when it wasn't holding his schoolbooks. With the exception of the winter months, a sweat mark burnished the back of his shirt whenever he removed the backpack. The camouflage pattern of the fabric was not the manufacturer's design, I discovered. It was Donny's doing. From his sweat, or his being pummeled by rain and snow and heat and blistering sun, or his dumping the backpack onto whatever texture and condition of earth happened to be underfoot after he yanked the padded straps off his shoulders and let it fall so that he could fully unleash the agile and animal-like side of him, the beast unburdened. His backpack was an appendage—ever-present, indispensable, taken for granted, and consequently prone to severe neglect. On the day that he set it down by the bleachers to join an impromptu game of touch football with no spectators around, I stood near the abandoned lump of stained canvas and leaned over, pretending that I was retying my sneaker, in order to get close to it. That's when I noticed that the camouflage pattern was not stamped into the fabric. It was an evolutionary seepage of stains bled out of Donny being Donny, which made me lean further toward the dark opening where the zipper hadn't been fully closed. Oh how it must smell in there if I could get close enough to that gap, that orifice. I didn't dare. What if he saw me? He'd understand instantly what I was up to and my life would be over.

Suitcase splayed on the bed, camphor fumes that I associated with Len, although it wasn't the smell of Len himself. Len was pretty much odorless. He showered a lot and used transparent glycerin soap and unscented deodorant. I came to count on his hygiene as much as I prayed for Donny's continual lack of it.

The sunlight was gaining strength, the dust motes so dense that I didn't recognize the world anymore and was panicking that my son and my granddaughter would be strangers to me when the plane touched down in a place that was unfamiliar to me. Where was it that Toby lived again? It would be on the boarding pass, I remembered, and if I should discover that it was a place Len and I hadn't been to, I'd make sure to ask for an airline tag to loop around the suitcase. If Len was right about the tags—and he was a master at being right about minor matters—the new addition will cause me to smile at some point in the future.

The flight attendant heaved the main door shut with such menacing authority that I wondered whether I was doomed to be forever sealed inside. I stood in front of my seat and twisted the plastic nozzle above me until a jet of cool air arrived at my face. I breathed it in slowly, deeply, from up close.

"Is this your first time?" the woman next to me asked. She was alone and more or less my age. I could tell by her neck.

"First time what?"

"Flying."

I sat down, crossed my arms over my chest, and stroked my shoulders with my hands. No wings that I could feel. "Not at all," I said. "It's been a while."

"Don't worry," she said. "They know what they're doing. What with technology and all. Soon we won't even need pilots to be flying these things."

She meant well and was wearing a huge diamond ring above a thick gold wedding band. I decided that she was happily married and had no designs on me, other than to make the time pass. Still, she could try to draw me into conversation, which I especially didn't want to do once we reached the altitude where the "fasten seatbelt" sign switched off. That's when I'd enter what Len called my private limbo zone. "You know," he said, "where you're between everything you've left behind and everything you're going to." I played the games at the back of the in-flight magazine, had cat naps, connected dots in my head. Len and I kept to ourselves until the captain announced, "We are beginning our final descent. Please fasten your seatbelts." Then we'd come to life for each other again.

"Care for my nuts?" the woman asked me halfway through the flight. "They're salted. I have to keep away from salt."

I asked her if she wanted to swap her nuts for my packet of Oreos.

"That's kind of you," she said. "I love Oreos, but I'm supposed to keep away from sugar."

Nothing salty, nothing sweet. What does she eat? Does she eat? I was tempted to look at her to see how skinny she had to be based on the math, but then she might start talking to me or, God forbid, assuming I was drawn to her in an animal-chemical-sex kind of way. I accepted her nuts, making sure that our fingers didn't touch. "Thank you," I said and turned my head back toward the seat in front of me. There were no video screens on the seatback above the tray table. Nothing to engage me, except a few tufts of red hair spilling over the seatback of the passenger in front of me. I peered through the crack between the seats, hoping to get a better look at the redhead. Nothing moved. The passenger must have been asleep.

When we landed, I offered to remove the woman's luggage from the overhead bin.

"That's kind of you," she said, "but I checked all my luggage. Four large pieces. I've been away for a while."

By the time I pulled my carry-on from the overhead bin and positioned it in front of me in the corridor, she was five exiting passengers in front of me. Part of me was glad that we managed to keep to ourselves during the flight. Another part regretted that I didn't get a snippet of her story, or find out who the passenger in front of me was, what with all that red hair. Then again, it was better this way. No need to get all obsessive about strangers.

The signs for the baggage claim area were many and clear, all with arrows pointing downward, indicating a lower level straight ahead. I followed them until I reached the escalator, where I kicked my suitcase onto the grillwork of the moving step in front of me, hurrying onto the one behind it before the two steps split along their fault line. Grabbing the rubber handrail to steady myself, I looked down and saw Toby and Lydia waiting for me at the bottom of the escalator, not at baggage claim as they'd instructed me. Still, I recognized them and, during the descent, remembered a much younger Lydia running up the down escalator at the mall to hug me around my legs when I took her shopping. But this was a much older version of Lydia. She wouldn't run up a down escalator to embrace her grandfather. I'd topple over. We were all too old for so many things. The two escalator steps I occupied were beginning their curl underneath the ramp. I positioned myself to make a graceful exit onto ground level. Mission accomplished, although the luggage tag on the handle of the suitcase I'd been fiddling with snapped off.

"Welcome, Dad!" Toby said, reaching for my suitcase. "Let me take that for you."

"That's okay, son. I've got it."

He wrapped his fingers around mine and gently pried them off. I relented without a fuss. He was being kind. Lydia gripped my arm above the elbow and steered me toward the exit. "That's okay, dear," I said. "I can manage." How bossy she could be. Four days at ground level with them. Too much? Too little? What were we wanting from each other? I put the severed luggage tag into my pants pocket. "I'll reattach it later," I thought. "It'll give me something to do when I'm restless. If Len were here, he'd make me smile right now. But he's not here, damn him."

Arrived at the house, Toby led me past the kitchen and down a foyer with numerous closed doors. He opened the one at the far end. "Voilà," he said. "Your private quarters. Make yourself at home. The chest of drawers is empty. Plenty of hangers in the closets, but don't take too long. We'll be eating in about a half-hour." He left me there.

ALONE IN MY private quarters, bright and spacious, furnished like a deluxe studio apartment (minus kitchenette): two plush armchairs, a sofa, magazines and books arranged fanlike on side and coffee tables, and a full-size bed. The layers of frilly pillow shams against the headboard clearly not the work of the Toby that I know. A new woman in his life? I continued to survey the room. Where's the door to the bathroom in all of this? I'll need to pee at least once in the night.

After I stationed my suitcase between the two sets of double doors of the closets, I removed the luggage tag from my pocket. Parting the other tags on the suitcase handle as if I were preparing to shuffle a deck of cards, I reattached the tag in the center and pushed the mass of other tags back together until they formed a tight deck, but not before repeating where I was: Madison, Wisconsin. Madison Madison Madison. Voices coming from the kitchen, but not the words being said, only pitches and syncopations that are familiar, familial. I slipped off my shoes and sat on the small L-shaped sofa, making sure not to rest my head on the wall. Don't want to leave grease marks. My left knee was acting up, which happens every so often, although I can't figure out what triggers it, and my eyes were aching with fatigue.

Garlic and spurts of laughter were coming from the kitchen. I opened my eyes to a sun casting a coral sunset hue on the unfamiliar objects in this unfamiliar room. For how long did I doze off? Then the call came, the one I'd heard throughout my life—from my mother, from Donny's mother, from Len; the call I myself made time and time again, a simple ritualistic call with the authority to bring all individual activity to a halt and demand that the announcement be heeded immediately.

"Dinner's ready!"

Where am I again? I remembered: with my son and granddaughter a corridor away. In Madisonwisconsin. Toby Toby Toby Lydia Lydia Lydia. Yes. They're nearby, waiting for me. My Tobeleh. My Matchstick.

"Coming," I shouted. "Just putting a few things in order."

I tensed up in the dark narrow foyer, much like I do when the MRI machine is about to suck me inside for the latest neurodegenerative trends in my brain to be scanned. The result is always the same—inconclusive—but I schedule follow-up visits, even after reaching the insurance ceiling and having to pay out of pocket. Surely something definitive will show up in all that buzzing and humming and darkness. Isn't that the point of science? To extrapolate certainty?

The voices in the kitchen grew louder, stronger. Lots of laughter (and a scent of rosemary). Are they laughing without me? Because of me? What do I want from them right now and forever? To receive the spillover of my fullness? Fill up my emptiness? Quietly accept my slipping away?

"Everything okay, Grandpa?"

"On my way!"

Time to enter into the light of the kitchen. Into the bustling love of Toby Toby Toby Lydia Lydia Lydia, to let them help me fall back into step, regain some traction, while there's time.

The End

ABOUT THE AUTHOR

BRETT SHAPIRO is an American writer and the author of two novels: *Late in the Day* (2022) and *Those around Him* (2019). His best-selling memoir *l'Intruso* was published in Italy, where he lived for 25 years, and it later became an award-winning film and theatrical production. He is the author of two children's books, one of which was the recipient of Austria's National Book Award. His short stories have been performed in theatres throughout Italy. He is a veteran writer for the United Nations and currently lives by the beach on Cape Cod and in Florida.

ABOUT ATMOSPHERE PRESS

Founded in 2015, Atmosphere Press was built on the principles of Honesty, Transparency, Professionalism, Kindness, and Making Your Book Awesome. As an ethical and author-friendly hybrid press, we stay true to that founding mission today.

If you're a reader, enter our giveaway for a free book here:

SCAN TO ENTER
BOOK GIVEAWAY

If you're a writer, submit your manuscript for consideration here:

SCAN TO SUBMIT
MANUSCRIPT

And always feel free to visit Atmosphere Press and our authors online at atmospherepress.com. See you there soon!